Rogan moved closer, until he could feel her body heat.

"I've no use for seers, Alison Blair. And even less for their servants."

Aly swallowed hard, and he could see the agitation suddenly take hold of her. Still she kept her gaze fixed on his. "I'm no one's servant."

"And yet here you stand at their beck and call."

"It's my duty."

"And now you've done it and it's past time for me to be doing mine," he muttered thickly, grabbing her upper arm to steer her out of his house.

But as he touched her, something unexpected happened. Something dazzling. An arc of what could have been lightning jolted between them. White-hot heat—and something more—sizzled in the air, and Rogan released her instantly.

He knew that sizzle and flash.

He'd felt it just once before.

For his Destined Mate.

But she had been dead for hundreds of years.

Books by Maureen Child

Silhouette Nocturne

*Eternally #4
*Nevermore #10
*Vanished #57

Silhouette Desire

**Bargaining for King's Baby #1857
**Marrying for King's Millions #1862
**Falling for King's Fortune #1868
High-Society Secret Pregnancy #1879
Baby Bonanza #1893
An Officer and a Millionaire #1915

*Guardians
**Kings of California

MAUREEN CHILD

is a California native who loves to travel. Every chance they get, she and her husband are taking off on another research trip. An author of more than sixty books, Maureen loves a happy ending and still swears that she has the best job in the world. She lives in Southern California with her husband, two children and a golden retriever with delusions of grandeur.

USA TODAY Bestselling Author

MAUREEN CHILD

∞

VANISHED

Silhouette Books

nocturne™

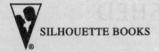

SILHOUETTE BOOKS

ISBN-13: 978-0-373-61804-0
ISBN-10:   0-373-61804-2

Recycling programs
for this product may
not exist in your area.

VANISHED

Printed in U.S.A.

Dear Reader,

The setting in *Vanished* is very special to me. Ireland is my favorite place in the world. The people are warm and friendly, the country itself is more beautiful than I can describe and with every breath you take, you can almost taste the magic in the air.

On our last trip to Ireland, my husband and I rented a cottage in County Mayo. It sits at the foot of the Partry Mountains and the windows of the cottage open up to amazing views of Lough Mask. For several weeks, we settled into the village, got to know the people and in general had a wonderful time.

So when it came time to write *Vanished*, I just knew I had to set my story there.

Rogan Butler is an immortal Guardian who died in the service of the last high king of Ireland, Brian Boru, in 1014. He now defends Ireland and humanity from the demon incursion.

Alison Blair is a hereditary member of the Guardian Society, a group of people who have kept faith with the immortals for centuries—helping where they can and keeping all-important records.

But not every Guardian wants the Society's help. When Alison Blair turns up on his doorstep, Rogan wants nothing to do with her. Despite being drawn to her, he keeps his distance, until her sister disappears and Alison has no one but Rogan to turn to.

I hope you enjoy *Vanished* as much as I enjoyed writing it! And if you're ever lucky enough to get to Ireland, be sure to visit the village of Tourmakeady.

Happy reading,

Maureen

To the Staunton family at Knight's Cottage

Shanvallyard, Tourmakeady, Ireland

Thank you for your warm welcome

And for making our stay in Ireland so memorable.

Chapter 1

In Ireland, two thousand people vanish every year.

The Irish countryside was quiet and the darkness was absolute, as it could only be far from the lights of a city. Here, beside the narrow road that led to Westport, the night felt empty, but for the squares of lamplight in the distance, marking the places where farmhouses stood in silence.

In the grassy field, ancient tombstones tipped and tilted crazily as if they'd been dropped from heaven and left to stand as they fell. Trees bent in the wind, and their bare limbs clattered like a muttered conversation. A fairy mound rose from the ground and lay littered with wildflowers that looked black and white in the starlight. A sigh of something ancient whispered in the darkness, and far away, a dog moaned into the quiet.

A young woman stood in the center of the stones, as she'd been told. She waited, impatiently checking her wristwatch and shrugging away the superstitious twitch at the base of her spine. The stones were eerie enough during the day, but at night, when the sky was black but for the stars, the woman half expected ghosts to rise up and chase her out of their graveyard.

The woman shivered again at the thoughts jostling through her mind and shrugged deeper into her coat. There was nothing to fear, after all. Hadn't she grown up here? Didn't she know this road to Westport well enough to travel it in her sleep?

No, the only thing to worry her was that maybe the man she waited for had forgotten his promise to meet her. Maybe he was with someone else. Maybe…

"Darlin'," a deep voice whispered from close by. "I knew you'd come. I've been waiting for you."

She whirled around, a smile of welcome on her face. Something blacker than the darkness rushed at her. She screamed as a howl lifted into the air, and a moment later the cemetery lay empty in the night.

* * *

"What was *that?*" Alison Blair stopped dead and felt the small hairs at the back of her neck stand straight up.

The long, undulating howl still quavered in the air as she stared back down the road into the darkness.

"A dog, no doubt," the guard at the wrought-iron gate muttered in an Irish accent so thick it almost sounded as though he were speaking Gaelic.

"Scary dog," Aly muttered, turning back to watch as the big man studied her ID card. Frowning, she said, "It's not a forgery, you know."

He flicked a glance at her from under thick black brows, and she deliberately lifted her chin and met that stony stare with one of her own.

The man nodded in approval, then said, "There'll be hell to pay when the boss hears you've come."

"I know." As a member of the Guardian Society, Aly knew she would be as welcome here as a flu virus.

Even in the best of circumstances, Immortal Guardians weren't exactly the most hospitable people in the universe. They lived alone, worked in secret and protected their real identities from a world filled with people who would never understand.

Chosen at the moment of their death, the Guardians were given the choice of either moving on to whatever awaited them or accepting immortality and the task of defending humankind against the demon threat. The Guardians were devoted to doing their duty and in general preferred to do that duty with as little interference as possible.

Both from humanity and the Society.

The Society had existed as long as the Guardians themselves. Generation after generation the families who belonged to the Society had worked with the Guardians. Some of those Guardians reluctantly accepted the help of the Society, and some…didn't.

Rogan Butler, Irish warrior and a Guardian centuries old, fell into the latter category.

"As you can see," she said, reaching out to take the papers identifying herself as a Society member, "I am who I say I am, and I need to see Rogan Butler immediately."

"He'll not be happy."

"Fortunately," she said, "his happiness is not my responsibility."

She really should have waited until morning to come and beard the lion in his den or lair, she thought, turning her gaze to the two-storied manor house beyond the iron gate. But she'd flown in from Chicago expressly for this meeting, and she wanted it over and done with.

Of course, if her sister Casey had bothered to come along with her, Aly thought, she wouldn't be feeling so on edge. Strength in numbers, after all. But though she'd been happy enough to come along on the trip to Ireland, Casey had insisted on re-minding Aly that *she* wasn't a member of the Society. Casey had been the first member of the Blair family for centuries to *not* pick up her here-ditary calling.

And Aly remembered clearly the argument they'd had at the B and B just an hour ago.

"You could come with me just for moral support," Alison had said as she and her sister fought for space in front of the tiny bathroom mirror.

"Oh, right. That sounds like a good time." Casey tugged at the hem of her V-necked, red T-shirt until it showed just enough of her breasts, then smiled at her elder sister. "Look, Aly, this secret-agent thing is your deal. Not mine. I didn't join the Society, remember?"

Aly scowled, hip-checked Casey out of her way and pulled her long, thick blond hair into a ponytail at the base of her neck. Then she wrapped the elastic band with a dark blue scarf and let the ends trail across her shoulders. Staring into the mirror, she gave herself the once-over before answering her sister. Dark blue jacket, white button-down oxford shirt tucked into dark blue jeans and black boots. She looked fine. Businesslike but casual. Friendly but stern.

Then she rolled her eyes at her own thoughts and turned from the mirror to face Casey. "Yes, I remember that you didn't join the Society. I'm not asking you to be officially there. I was just looking for some company."

Casey muscled her way in front of Aly to check her own reflection again. She fluffed her short, dark blond hair and shrugged. "I don't know why you're so nervous about this. Rogan Butler isn't the first Guardian you've ever spoken to."

"True." Aly sat down on the edge of the bathtub, stretched out her legs and said, "But he's the first one who refused to talk to me on the phone. And our psychics refused to call the Ireland office so one of their members could deliver the message in person, so…"

Casey shook her head, fluffed her hair again and leaned in to smooth another layer of dark red lipstick on her mouth. When she was finished, she straightened up, smiled at her reflection and said, "Imagine that. Jealous psychics. Aren't they supposed to be above all that?"

"They should be," Aly admitted. "But you know how they are. Especially Reginald."

"You're defining the reasons I didn't want to join the Society, Aly," Casey said. "No way do I want to spend all my time trying to soothe cosmic egos."

And maybe she had a point, Aly thought now,

grimly steeling herself for her meeting with the Irish bully known as Rogan Butler.

"Well, then," the guard said, his musical accent rising up and down as he spoke. "I'll get the gate. Just drive on up to the manor. You'll be met."

Aly got back into her car and swallowed hard as the guard unlocked the gates and swung them open. She steered her car, absentmindedly noting the tidy lawn and the spill of golden lamplight pouring from the lead glass windows of the manor and lying across the gravel drive.

Aly's stomach pitched a little, and she told herself to get a grip. She wouldn't allow a Guardian to make her nervous. As a member of the Society, she had every right—no, a *duty*—to give him the information the Chicago psychics had discovered.

She parked the car directly in front of the double doors and stepped out, pocketing the keys. Grabbing her purse, she headed for the house and stopped dead when those double doors were pulled open and a giant of a man stood backlit against the entryway.

Rogan Butler.

It had to be.

His shoulders were broad, his hips were narrow and his legs were long and thick with muscles. His black hair hung loose past his shoulders and lifted in the icy wind like a battle flag. As she watched, he folded massive arms across an impressive chest and stared down at her.

"Alison Blair?" His accent was, if possible, even thicker than that of the man at the gate. And his voice was like thunder. Deep and powerful.

"Yes." Apparently his security man had alerted him to her identity. "And you're Rogan Butler."

"I am. Why've you come?"

So much for niceties. "Because you wouldn't take my phone call."

"I had no wish to speak with you. I still don't."

Limned in lamplight, his features were in shadow, but Aly didn't have to see his face to know he was frowning. She could *feel* his scowl, his irritation, flowing from him in thick waves.

Her nerves jittered a little, and for one moment she wished she were anywhere but there. But there hadn't been another available Chicago Society member to make the trip, and the Society psychics so guarded their "visions" they hadn't wanted to call Ireland and get one of the local members to deliver the message.

So, here she was. Facing down one of the most legendary of the Guardians, and she had to fight to keep from getting back into her car and driving away. But if she did that, she'd never live it down.

"The Society will find no welcome here." He said it briskly, as if already dismissing her.

"We're not your enemy, you know," Aly countered quickly. "We're on the same side. Fighting the same war."

"Is that what you think, then?" He came down one of the steps and stopped. "And how many demons have you fought, Alison Blair?"

"None, but—"

"A thousand and more demons have fallen beneath my blade. All without the help you've come so far to offer."

"The Society is—"

"Useless?" he offered.

"There's no reason to be insulting, either." She walked toward him, forcing her feet to move despite the fact that her muscles were locked up as if desperately trying to keep her in one place. "I've come with an important message and I'm not leaving until I've delivered it."

He blew out a breath and came down the remaining steps until he stood on the drive right in front of her. Aly tipped her head back to stare up into his eyes. Green, she thought. A shining, clear green that seemed almost iridescent in the pale light. His jaw was hard and square and bristled with a day's growth of whiskers. His mouth was firm and flattened into a disapproving line, and his heavy black brows were drawn down on his forehead.

He was, without a doubt, the most gorgeous man she'd ever seen.

And despite the fact that his irritation still simmered in the air around him, Aly felt a small twist of something hot and needy bubble into life inside her.

Which was just unacceptable.

"Fine, then deliver your message and be on your way."

"If you don't mind, I'd rather not discuss this outside."

"You're a prissy little thing, aren't you?"

"Prissy? *Prissy?*" Narrowing her eyes on him, she said, "I'm an official representative of the Guardian Society. I've just spent twelve hours in a plane to get here. Then I had to rent a car and try not to nod off at the wheel while I forced myself to drive on the wrong side of the road." He opened his mouth as if to speak, but she kept right on, feeling her sense of righteous indignation build up and spill over. "The hotel lost my reservation, and my sister and I had to search for a local B and B. After getting to our room, instead of having a meal or taking a much-needed nap—or even, God help me, going for a drink with my sister—I got in that blasted car with the steering wheel on the wrong side of the damn thing and drove straight here, only to be treated like a common criminal by your security thugs and now to be insulted by *you*. If it weren't in humanity's best interests to give you this message, believe me when I say I'd as soon keep my mouth shut, turn around and go home."

When she finally ran down, Aly took a breath and

waited for him to order her off his property. Fine. She hadn't handled her first official assignment very well, but she'd like to have seen anyone else handle it better.

"Well, then," he said after an impossibly long moment, "you'd best come inside and give me this all-important message."

He stepped back and waved an arm, silently inviting her to precede him into the house. Lifting her chin, she did just that, taking the steps slowly as jet lag began taking its toll.

She stepped into the entryway and paused just for a moment to take a quick look around. Polished wood floors gleamed in the lamplight, and colorful rugs were scattered along the narrow hall that stretched off to the back end of the house. To her left was a formal sitting room and to her right what looked to be a library. A fire roared in the stone hearth, wall sconces shaped like oil lanterns threw soft, electric light onto the paneled walls and over-stuffed furniture in shades of forest green and burgundy offered comfort. The walls were lined with bookshelves, and every tabletop was crowded with towering piles of hardcover books.

She loved the room immediately.

"This way," he said and walked past her into the clearly masculine room. Making directly for an escritoire, he opened the carved doors to reveal crystal decanters and drinking glasses. "You'll have a drink, then tell me."

"No, thank you."

"You look as though you're ready to keel over," he said, dismissing her argument as he poured amber-colored liquor into two glasses. "A little of the Irish will set you straight in no time."

He came back to her and handed her one of the glasses. She took a sniff and frowned. "I don't really drink whiskey."

Tossing his own drink back, he swallowed, then said, "This is Paddy's. It's like no other. Drink it down and tell me what you've come to say."

Easier to do as he wanted rather than fight him on something that didn't seem very important. Mimicking his action, Aly took a breath, lifted her glass and poured the liquor down her throat in a straight shot.

Instantly, fire bloomed inside and stole her breath. Gasping a little, she handed the glass back to him and slapped one hand to her chest. "Thanks," she managed to say when she was able to choke out a word.

Rogan set the glasses down onto the nearest tabletop and watched the woman who'd come all the way from the United States to see him. He had no use for the Guardian Society. He was a warrior and had managed, since the day of his death in

1014, to battle demons without the help of those who thought themselves to be a part of the Guardian legacy.

There were others, friends of his, who had made use of the Society from time to time, but Rogan believed a man worked better when he was alone, a hard lesson he'd learned centuries ago and one he kept always in the forefront of his mind. He needed nothing from anyone and wanted no "help" in performing his duty.

He'd been ready to order Alison Blair off his property when she'd found her spine and given him a dressing-down like no one had dared to do in centuries. And with that outburst of temper, she'd won a glimmer of admiration from him, a glimmer strong enough to allow her into his home—however briefly.

"Say what you must, then, and be on your way."

"If this is Irish hospitality, it's sadly lacking."

"Ah, but you're not a guest now, are you?" He turned from her, walked to his favorite chair and sat down, kicking both legs out in front of him and crossing his feet at the ankles. "You say you've a mission to fulfill. Then fulfill it and be done."

He watched her and saw anger flash in her blue eyes quickly before she was able to hide it from him. Instantly, he wondered what kind of woman it was who buried her emotions so completely. The women he'd known in his life had all worn their hearts in the open, risking bruising and hurt but unable to do anything else.

And as that thought sneaked into his consciousness, it was followed by an ancient memory, one he rarely allowed himself to entertain. The image of a woman rose up in his mind. Her long, black hair flying about her head in the sea wind. Her blue eyes shining, laughing. Her mouth curved in welcome for him. And before he could pause a moment to enjoy them, the images shifted, changed, becoming the nightmare that haunted him still from time to time.

Rogan shut off his thoughts with the ease of long practice and turned his focus to the woman still standing across the room from him. Irritated suddenly, he said, "Sit, will you? And say what you've come to say."

Her boot steps were muffled on the thick carpets as she moved to the chair nearest him. She perched on the edge of the chair, folded her hands in her lap and squeezed until her knuckles turned white. That was the only sign of her agitation, and again Rogan was forced to admire her self-control.

While the fire crackled and hissed in the hearth and tree limbs driven by the ever-present Irish wind scratched at the windowpanes, she watched him steadily for a long moment. Then she said softly, "One of the Chicago seers has had a vision."

He gave her a half smile. "Wouldn't that be a seer's job?"

She didn't answer that jibe. Instead, she began to give him a bloody lecture.

Her surprisingly prim voice carried just over the hiss of the fire. "As you know, the Society psychics are some of the most powerful in the world. Society membership is hereditary. For centuries, the same families have protected the secrets of the Guardians and done all we can to help you in your fight against the demon incursion—"

Scowling, he snapped, "If you've come only to give me a history lesson, Alison Blair, I'll remind you I've been living history for longer than you would care to consider."

She frowned right back at him. "Each generation," she said, a bit louder than before, as if daring him to try to talk over her, "more psychics are born into the Society, and with each generation one or two of those seers has incredible strength."

"And would you be one of those with the power of second sight, darlin'?"

"I would not," she said, pausing just long enough to give him an irritated nod. "I have some psychic abilities but nothing in the range of the seers. Reginald, the seer who sent me here, is extremely powerful. His visions are always clear. His messages have saved countless lives, including those of your fellow Guardians."

"We're immortal, love," he said, hooking his arms behind his head in a lazy move that belied the tension coiling in the pit of his belly. "We've no lives to be saved."

"Immortal, yes, but you can be desperately wounded, taking years to recover."

Annoyed, he said, "You're not telling me anything I don't already know."

"I'm trying to impress on you just how important it is for you to listen to Reginald's message."

"Then deliver it, by damn."

She drew her head back and stared at him. In the firelight, her blue eyes shone with the reflection of the flames until it looked as though light were dancing within her. Her mouth was tight, her posture was so stiff it was as if she'd a poker stuffed down the back of her jacket and her knotted fingers were almost white with her repressed fury.

"You are the rudest man I've ever met."

He brushed that aside. "Ah, but I'm not a man, am I? Besides, you've not seen rude yet, Alison Blair, but if you don't get on with it, you very well may."

She ground her teeth together as if trapping inside words that wanted to spill from her mouth. It was almost entertaining to watch. Almost. But time was flying by and Rogan had no interest in sitting by the fire with a woman, no matter how attractive he found her; it was past time for him to be out on the hunt.

"Fine, then," she said after a long moment's

pause. "Reginald has seen the rise of a very dangerous power. Here. Soon."

He laughed. And when her features stiffened in shock, he laughed harder. "*This* is the so important message? Your seer's looked beyond the veil and seen trouble, has he?" He rubbed his jaw and pretended to give the matter great thought. "What kind of trouble do you think, then? Could it be…*demons?*"

"Are you really so arrogant you can't accept help when it's offered?"

"I don't need your help. Or apparently the help of your gifted seer. I know there's trouble, don't I?" He stood up and looked down at her from his great height. "Demons are nothing new to me, Alison Blair."

"This isn't an ordinary demon," she said quietly, as if she were measuring each word and weighting it down with patience before speaking it. "Reginald saw an extreme amount of energy surrounding the nearest portal. He says that it's building daily and that there's a danger beyond the normal threat."

Rogan scowled at her and thought about the seer's message. He'd known for days now that something unusual was happening. There had been reported cases of people mysteriously vanishing all over Ireland. And there'd been more demon activity lately as well. He didn't like any of it.

She stood up and that flicker of admiration, respect he'd felt for her earlier, sharpened a bit. She wasn't put off by his great size or by the reputation and legends surrounding him. He'd give her points for foolhardy bravery if nothing else.

"I'll do what I can to look into the seer's vision," he said, though it cost him. He didn't want to take orders from a psychic. Nor from a woman.

"Thank you. I'll make my report to the Society."

"You do that."

"You don't have to like me or the Society," she said, clearly irritated that he wasn't more appreciative of the effort she'd gone to in delivering this oh-so-very-vague message. "But you could at least show some respect."

"Respect?" His voice boomed out before he could stop it. "For psychics and seers who sit in the background and make proclamations? Who have visions too late to help? Who see things that can't be changed and then demand reverence for their faulty abilities?" Rogan moved in closer, until he could feel her body heat reaching out to him. Rage pounded in his brain and thundered through his veins.

"The psychics do their best," she countered, blindly defending the group that was her family's legacy. "Visions aren't always clear."

"Aye," he agreed, feeling the fury threaten to overcome him. "But they don't admit to mistakes, do they? No. They speak as if from the Mount and expect all to listen and revere. Well, I've no use for seers, Alison Blair. And even less use for their servants."

She swallowed hard and he could see agitation suddenly take hold of her. Still, she kept her gaze fixed with his. "I'm no one's servant."

"And yet here you stand, at their beck and call."

"It's my duty."

"And now you've done it, and it's past time for me to be doing mine," he muttered thickly, grabbing her upper arm to steer her out of his house.

But as he touched her, something unexpected happened, something dazzling. An arc of what could have been lightning jolted between them. White-hot heat and something more sizzled in the air, and Rogan released her instantly.

He knew that sizzle and flash.

He'd felt it just once before.

For his Destined Mate.

But she had been dead for hundreds of years.

Chapter 2

Casey tapped the toe of her shoe to the insistent beat of the traditional Irish music pouring out of the pub behind her. Even here on the sidewalk, the music was rich and full, making her consider going back inside despite how tired she was. With drums, pipes and fiddles, the small group of people huddled in a corner of the pub had the locals dancing and the tourists wishing they knew how to step dance.

Her first day in Ireland and already she was in love with the country. The cold, Irish wind buffeted her, the Guinness she'd drunk warmed her from the inside and fuzzed her jet-lagged mind into a kind of easy fog and the tidy streets of Westport made her feel safer than she ever had back home in Chicago. Even now, when it was nearly midnight, she wasn't worried to be alone on a street corner waiting for the taxi she'd called.

And, okay, maybe that was foolish, but she wasn't going to obsess about it. She'd stay in the light of the pub, within shouting distance of help, if she needed it. But she wouldn't. The people were all so friendly. She'd talked all night, tried a dance step or two and then laughed like a loon when she hadn't been able to keep up with an elderly man who, though he had to be at least a hundred years old, was as light on his toes as a ballet dancer.

The night had been a great welcome to Ireland, one her sister had missed. "Poor Aly. Off being the dutiful little soldier when she could have been here having fun."

In the pub, the music abruptly shifted from a wildly paced tune called "Finnegan's Wake" to something slow and sad and just a little dreamy. Casey sighed as the notes soared into the night and told herself that this sense of freedom she was experiencing was exactly why she hadn't wanted to accept her legacy and join the Society.

For centuries, her family had served the Guardians. And what had they gotten for it? Very little. Heck, the Guardians themselves barely tolerated Society members. The pay was stingy, the respect was almost nonexistent and because you took an oath of secrecy, you couldn't even tell your friends what you did for a living!

"No, thank you," she muttered as if she were having the familiar argument with her elder sister. Aly had been working for the Society since she was eighteen. She'd been the "good" daughter, the obedient one, the one who did whatever their parents expected of her. She'd been sucked into the secretive Society and had immersed herself in the traditions and rules, much as their parents had. Aly bought into the mentality of serving humanity and helping the Guardians, and Casey had never been able to change her mind.

Well, for Casey it was different. She'd never been convinced that the "demon threat" was all that horrifying. After all, the demons had been trying to take over humankind for thousands of years and they hadn't succeeded yet. How terrifying could they possibly be? No. She was more convinced that it was Guardian propaganda that had kept the Society members in practical servitude for centuries.

"They're no better than cosmic bullies," she muttered. "Ordering us around like we're peasants, then ignoring us when it suits them. Ten to one, Rogan Butler didn't even let Aly get close enough to deliver her stupid message."

Shaking her head, Casey determinedly turned

her mind from her sister and the Guardian she was sent to meet. After all, it was *so* not her problem. She was here to enjoy herself, and that's just what she was going to do.

"But where is the stupid taxi?"

Another gust of icy ocean air blew in off Clew Bay and wrapped itself around Casey like a long-lost lover. She shivered a little and wished she'd worn a heavier jacket. But the black leather had gone so well with her outfit that she hadn't wanted to spoil her look.

A voice drifted to her, and she turned toward the sound. Just across the wide street, a three-foot-high stone wall separated the road from the Carrowbeg River. The length of the wall was dotted with trees and old-fashioned streetlamps that offered more in ambiance than in actual lighting.

She listened harder, but when she didn't hear anything more, she brushed it off and again stared down the street, willing her taxi to appear.

"Help me..."

There it was again. A sigh almost lost in the rush of the river and the whisper of the wind, never mind the music still erupting inside the pub. Frowning, she thought about stepping into the pub to get assistance but then reconsidered. If she was imagining the call—and chances of that were good, since she was so tired she could hardly stand upright—she'd look like a fool.

Quickly, she looked up and down the street and then crossed the road in a fast trot that had her boot steps echoing softly around her. Clutching the edges of her jacket together, she walked up to the short stone fence and stared down into the fast-moving river. She didn't see anyone, didn't hear anyone, so she must be more jet-lagged than she'd thought.

Despite the streetlamps, it was darker here than it had been in front of the noisy pub. Shadows were everywhere, crouching in patches of deeper black, and Casey was suddenly uneasy. She glanced around her but saw no one. Nothing. Yet the sensation of being watched was so real, so bone-deep certain she couldn't shake it. A chill snaked along her spine. She looked back at the pub and took comfort in the bright splash of light streaming through the wide front window. She wasn't alone. Help was just a shout away.

"You've come…"

A voice. Deep, musical, mesmerizing. Casey pulled in a long, deep breath, then let it slide slowly from her lungs. She swayed and felt her head go light, as if a fog had slipped into her mind, shrouding her thoughts, wrapping her brain in a haze that grew thicker with every beat of her heart. She shook her head, tried to clear it, but the fog remained, thick, warm.

"Who are you? Where are you?" She held her

breath and waited for that compelling, soothing, completely sexual voice again.

"Ah, darlin'…I've been waitin'…"

"Yes," she whispered, licking her lips, sighing as unseen fingers moved over her body, stroking, touching, enticing.

A shadow lifted from the earth, twisting in the wind, contorting itself, writhing as if fighting to come into existence.

Casey couldn't move.

Couldn't speak.

She could only watch, breathlessly.

And the dark came alive. A howl lifted into the air, and a moment later the river walk was empty.

"I don't know what you're trying to do," Aly said, rubbing her upper arm with her free hand as if trying to ease a bone-deep burn. Where he'd grabbed her, her skin still tingled, still hummed with the unexpected charge of electricity that had arced between them.

She'd been a member of the Society for more than ten years. She spent her days researching the different Guardians and the legends and tales that surrounded them. She knew all about the myth of Destined Mates. And she'd read about the bonding that happened between them, the link that sprang to life at first touch and how that link became stronger over time.

Well, no, thank you.

"I've no idea what you're blatherin' about," Rogan muttered and didn't look any too happy about the situation himself.

Although, he hadn't been exactly a cheery man since he'd first opened his door for her. So, that probably didn't mean anything.

"I know the legends," she said, just to make sure he knew exactly how she felt about this. She wanted no mistakes, no misunderstandings. She was here to do a job, see a little of Ireland, then go home. "The Destined Mate thing? I know all about it, and you should know, I'm so not interested."

"Don't recall asking you to be interested."

She ignored that, as she ignored the sizzle in her blood and the near-overpowering sense of *recognition* her soul was feeling. No, no, no. "I've got a life, thanks, and I'm not looking to subjugate myself to some medieval warrior who doesn't even know the meaning of common courtesy. And now that I've done what I was sent here to do, I'm gone."

"Be on your way, then." He swung one muscular arm out in a wide arc, showing her the way out as if she couldn't remember it for herself. "No one's keepin' you."

"Fine." Everything in her yearned to stay. Feelings she didn't want crowded her mind, her heart, but she ruthlessly shut them down. Clearly, she'd been spending too much time at work and not enough time building a social life. If she could be this attracted to a crabby, overbearing Guardian, she really needed to get out more.

She turned on her heel and started for the front door. Just as she stepped into the entryway, though, she looked back at him. The fire crackled behind him, flames dancing in the hearth. Lamplight fell down onto him, making the black of his hair gleam almost blue. Those pale green eyes of his sparkled and shone with a glint of fury she hadn't noticed a moment before, and his full mouth was flattened into a grim slash.

God, he was amazing. Her body burned, but her mind was in control. And she was glad to see that he was no happier about that little jolt of something sizzling than she was. Then they could both ignore whatever it had been and go on with their lives. As it should be.

"Good luck with your demon hunting."

He folded his arms over that incredibly broad chest and muttered, "And you go back to your seer. Tell him I've no interest in anything he has to say."

She left him there in that wonderful room and told herself as she went that the buzzing in her blood had nothing to do with his touch.

After Alison Blair left, Rogan found he couldn't settle. His own home, the place he'd lived in for more than two hundred years, felt like a prison cell. It was as if the walls were closing in on him and air was too hard to come by. Damn woman should never have come.

The blasted Society had had no business sending her to him. He hadn't taken their calls, had he? Wasn't that plain enough that he'd no wish to hear from them? He prowled the confines of his library and found no pleasure in the books he'd collected over the lengthy span of his lifetime. He slapped both hands onto the Connemara marble mantel and stared down into the flames leaping and dancing in the hearth. Shadows flickered and lights shifted, and in the fire's depths he saw Alison Blair's face again and the surprise in her eyes when his touch had sparked off feelings neither of them wanted.

"Blast the woman," he muttered, feeling the hot, roiling ball of fury build in his gut and churn viciously. And as he closed his eyes to the image of her, he made a solemn vow. "I'll not do it again. I'll not be led by my cock for the amusement of the Fates."

And just saying the words aloud refocused his strength. Reminded him of who and what he was. Rogan Butler. Guardian. Warrior. And the softness of a woman had no place in his life—his was a world of blood and death.

That thought spurred him into action. He wasn't a man to stand still. Pushing away from the fireplace, he strode from the room, his long legs moving quickly, silently through the house. What he needed right now was a battle. Clean. Simple. He gathered his weapons, threw on his coat and went on the hunt.

As Rogan moved through the bitter, cold night, his long black coat slapping around his legs, he searched for a telltale swirl of demonic energy that would steer him in the right direction. Trace signatures left behind when a demon entered our dimension were invisible to humans, but to Guardians they appeared as faint washes of color.

"There you are, you bastard," he murmured, as his gaze caught a faint swirl of deep orange streaking through the stand of woods at the edge of Lough Mask.

The bitter taste of it was on the wind, and he turned, lifting his face, scenting his prey. His senses honed to a keen edge, Rogan sprinted soundlessly through the woods. The surface of Lough Mask looked like tarnished silver lying beneath a sliver of moon. The stars shone brilliantly in a black sky but shed little light on the countryside.

But Rogan didn't need light for his work. This he knew better than anyone else alive. He was one of the oldest Guardians, and he'd been fighting demons for what seemed an eternity. Scenting the air again, he smiled grimly and lost himself in the trees. His steps were silent, his breathing steady and hushed. His gaze swept the terrain he knew as well as he knew the layout of his own home.

This was his country. He'd lived and died in Ireland and chose to remain here as one of the Guardians who defended the island against demon encroachment. He was Irish to the bone, and this very ground was a part of him. He'd traveled the globe and never found another spot like this one. Always, he'd been drawn back here, to County Mayo, where Gaelic was still spoken, as it should be. The old ways were remembered here. Revered.

Here no farmer would think to run a tractor across a fairy mound—unwilling to risk angering the little people. Here trees were left to stand tall in the fields and crops were planted around them. Here ruins of castles echoed with the ghosts of warriors long dead.

And here his own memories both comforted and tormented him.

The wind on the water churned whitecaps that slapped at the surface of the lake and sounded like hundreds of cats lapping at cream. The trees around him bent and swayed. His eyes narrowed, and every one of his Guardian senses reached into the darkness. The scent was clear, but the faint wash of orange had dissipated in the wind.

A crack of a twig.

A hiss of breath.

Rogan spun about and pounced.

The burly demon had thought to sneak up on him and Rogan would have laughed at the very idea, but he was too busy, swinging a sword he had carried for eons. The very balance of the heavy blade felt a part of him, an extension of his arm as he whipped it through the air with such power the wind sang as it caressed the finely honed metal.

His blade hit home with a smack of steel against flesh. The demon howled in fury and pain and charged Rogan in desperation. Wild, burning eyes flashed in the darkness and long, lethal claws swiped at him. But Rogan was more than ready. He'd been bred to fight, and over the hundreds of years that had passed since his death, his abilities with a blade had become legendary—even among the Guardians.

The demon snarled, his jaw dropping to reveal jagged teeth nearly two inches long. The stench of demon blood fouled the air and Rogan hissed in a breath. His heart pounded frantically and his blood rushed. He dropped into a crouch, swinging his blade in another wide arc from which the demon leaped back to avoid. Minutes ticked past, and the wind around him tossed dirt and leaves into the air.

And Rogan hardly noticed. His focus was on his opponent. On the battle. He fought because it was his duty. Because a warrior was all he was.

Because he knew nothing else.

Again and again they clashed viciously. The

defender and the beast. "You should have stayed in hell, demon. There's no place in Ireland for the likes of you."

The demon spat at him, and its saliva mixed with blood, bubbling into a frothy acid on the ground at Rogan's feet. "Guardians are few and we are many."

Rogan leaped through the air, and as he came down, he brought the hilt of his sword crashing into the demon's skull. The solid hit staggered the beast, and it dropped to the earth, stunned. Rogan planted one boot on the small of its back and held it pinned to the ground while it cursed and screamed. In a moment he'd secure the bloody damn thing and cart it off back to the portal and its rightful dimension. Demons were hard to kill here on this plane. The most a Guardian could do was capture it and send it back to hell.

"Bastard!" The demon twisted and writhed in a futile effort to free itself. "You'll pay for this! I'll see to it! Armies of demons will descend on you and yours."

Rogan stepped heavier on the beast until it ran out of air to shout with. "Many you may be," he agreed, smiling now that the fight was ended, "but we'll outlast the lot of you."

And while his captive fought desperately to escape him, Rogan slid his sword into its scabbard and lifted his face to the night sky. Victory and one less demon to threaten humankind this night. He'd done his duty. Done what he was meant to do.

Yet still the emptiness inside him rattled as it had for too many years to count.

"Casey?" Aly called quietly and stepped into their shared bedroom at the Radharc na Oilean B and B on the banks of Lough Mask. There were two twin beds covered by handmade quilts in beautiful shades of blues and greens. A wide dormer window overlooked the fields stretching out behind the farmhouse, and the lamp on the small table between the beds gave off a soft, warm glow.

Along with enough light for Aly to see that Casey wasn't back yet.

A flicker of worry sputtered into life inside her, but Aly told herself to calm down. She closed the door behind her, crossed the room and stared out at the sweep of open fields that lay at the feet of the Partry Mountains. There wasn't enough moonlight to see much, but she made out the blurred white patches of the sheep huddling together in the field for warmth. The end of March in Ireland was cold, even for the animals used to the biting wind.

Turning back around, Aly frowned as she stared at her sister's empty bed but told herself that Casey was an adult, old enough to take care of herself. She'd be back before long and no doubt be lording it all over Aly for the good time she'd missed because she'd had to deal with Rogan Butler.

Just the thought of the man's name had Aly rubbing her arm again. She could swear she still felt his touch on her skin. Which was just weird.

Her heartbeat quickened a bit as she remembered the cold gleam in his clear green eyes as he touched her. He'd felt that buzz of something molten between them as well as she had. And he hadn't looked any happier about it than she was. Small consolation.

Sighing, she eased her suitcase off the bed, then stretched out atop the quilt. Not bothering to change into her pajamas, she lay in the soft glow of lamplight and stared up at the sloping ceiling. But she wasn't seeing the clean, white paint over the eaves of what had once been the attic of the working farmhouse.

Instead, she was seeing Rogan Butler, frowning at her. She heard the rolling music of his accent and the deep reverberation of his voice as it sizzled along her spine. She remembered every moment with him so clearly it was as if it had been etched into her brain.

"Now, isn't that a lovely thought?" No. It wasn't. She didn't want to think about him. Didn't want to consider what that hum of electric charge between them might have meant. And surely didn't want to see him again.

And yet...

His face filled her mind as her eyes closed and her body surrendered to the jet lag tugging at her.

Casey still hadn't returned by morning.

Aly fought down a cold lump of fear in her belly and told herself there would be an explanation. Car trouble, maybe. No. She was going to catch a cab. Then perhaps an accident. Oh, God. That wasn't a good thought.

She went downstairs at the crack of dawn, but since the B and B was situated on a working sheep farm, her hostess was already up and busy. Aly accepted a cup of coffee, got directions on how to get to the city of Westport, then climbed into her car and took off.

The bucolic Irish countryside did nothing to dispel the sense of urgency bubbling inside her. Something was desperately wrong. She felt it. Aly knew her sister, and though Casey liked to have a good time, she wasn't stupid. And she wasn't the kind of woman who would have gone home with a man she'd just met.

Which left only one possibility.

Casey was in some kind of trouble.

The owner of the B and B had made a couple of phone calls for her, checking in with the local hospitals, but there was no record of an American woman being treated or admitted. So fine. She wasn't in the hospital. But that didn't mean she couldn't be lying in a ditch somewhere and...

"Stop it," she told herself. She wasn't going to let her imagination take over. There would be a reasonable explanation for this. Maybe Casey hadn't been able to get a cab back and had stayed at a hotel in town. "But if she'd done that, she would have called to let me know."

The narrow road unwound in front of her like a black ribbon snaking through lush fields of green. On either side of the road, gorse bushes sprouted tiny yellow flowers in clusters so rich and thick that you couldn't see through them to the farms beyond. On her right, Lough Mask lay spread out into the distance, a watery sun splotching the gray surface with flashes of brilliance.

When a car headed toward her, Aly gulped in a breath and held it, steering her car as far over to the left as she could. The gorse bushes scraped at the car, and as the other driver passed, he lifted a hand in greeting and drove on.

Aly blew out that breath and took another. She couldn't imagine driving these roads all the time. It was terrifying. But at the moment, she had more to frighten her than tiny roads, careless drivers and the sheep that suddenly wandered out in front of her.

Stomping on the brake, Aly jerked to a stop and waited while the white-and-black sheep stared at her as if she were an intruder. And, hell, she was. She should never have come here, Society or not. And she certainly shouldn't have brought Casey with her.

Casey.

Honking her horn, Aly eased off the brake and crept up on the sheep as slowly as she could. But she didn't have the time to simply sit parked while the damn animal decided where it wanted to go. Clearly irritated, the sheep glared at her, then bounded across the road and Aly was once more flying down a narrow strip of asphalt, muttering unintelligible prayers as she went.

The local police, the Garda, weren't too concerned when Aly faced them down with tales of a missing sister. But she'd been all over Westport. She'd visited dozens of pubs, talked to whoever would listen and, nearly frantic, had finally discovered the place her sister had last been seen, a pub called the Sidhe, which sat on the corner of the main street, just across from the river that snaked alongside the bustling city.

And the waitress at the Sidhe remembered serving Casey. Even remembered her leaving. Alone. About twelve o'clock the night before. Then, it was as if she'd slipped into a hole in the earth.

"If you don't mind my sayin' so, miss," the

sergeant at the broad wood desk said with a smile, "you're worrying for naught. I'm sure your sister is simply enjoying her first trip to Ireland."

Aly bit down on her frustration. The man was trying to be nice, after all. "The question, Sergeant, is *where* is she enjoying herself?"

He gave her another smile that flashed briefly in his clear blue eyes. "Ah, well, now. She's an adult, isn't she? There's no sign of foul play. You've said yourself, the waitress at the Sidhe says she left under her own power, none the worse for wear."

Around her, the police station hummed with activity. Somewhere down the long, narrow hallway a woman was crying, and Aly hoped to heaven that wasn't an omen. She heard snatches of English mixed in with the musical sound of Gaelic. Burned coffee stained the air, and the sergeant in front of her had bread crumbs on his uniform jacket. It was as if she were outside herself, noticing all the little details of the room in a blind effort to keep calm. To keep from screaming that her sister was in trouble and no one was listening.

"Now, if you'd like to leave the number of where you're staying, I'll be sure to let you know if I learn anything."

"Sergeant," Aly tried again, desperate to make him do something to help her. "My sister and I are traveling together. Casey wouldn't simply disappear without telling me. She would know that I'd be worried." Calm. Collected. In control. Hysteria would only make him dismiss her entirely. "Something's happened to her, and I need you to help me look for her."

Sighing, he pulled a piece of paper in front of him, picked up a pen and, giving her a look that clearly said she was wasting his precious time, asked, "Will you tell me again what she looks like?"

"Yes." Aly didn't care if he didn't believe her. Didn't care if he was patronizing her. All that mattered was that he was filling out an official report. She dug out her wallet, produced a picture of her sister and handed it over.

"I can't promise you much, miss." He studied the photo of a smiling Casey for a long moment, then made notes in a tidy hand. "Your sister's a grown woman. She's been gone only overnight. For all you know, she's hunkered down in a hotel with one of the local lads, I'm sorry for saying so."

Aly bit down hard on her bottom lip, then said, "Casey's not like that. I'm telling you, something is wrong. I know it."

"Ah, well, then, we'll see what we can do."

While he wrote down everything she said, Aly looked around the station again. And this time, she noticed the pages tacked up to a bulletin board in the entrance. *Missing* notices. With pictures and descriptions of young men and women. They dotted the entire surface of the corkboard and filled Aly with trepidation.

If the Garda hadn't found any of those people…how would they find Casey?

Chapter 3

Rogan slipped through the countryside and made no more than a whisper of sound. A young moon gave fitful light as it slipped in and out of thick clouds rolling in from the sea. He moved with the stealthy grace he had learned over the long centuries of solitary battles. His gaze swept the darkness as he made his way across the open field, searching, always searching for the telltale energy traces that would lead him to a demon.

The wind was icy and tossed the branches of the trees into a tangle of limbs. But he hardly noticed. The night was home to him, the open land more easy on his soul than four walls could ever be. He belonged here, hunting. The scent of peat smoke from a nearby chimney came to him, and for one brief moment, memories crowded Rogan's mind. Memories of other times, when he'd roamed these very hills in the company of his brother warriors. Before he'd died. Before he'd begun his eternity on the hunt.

As a Guardian, Rogan was one of many. Chosen at the moment of their death to defend humanity from the demon threat, Guardians were immortal. And with the gift of long life came other gifts. All of them were telepathic, able to read the minds of the humans they protected. Some of the Guardians had other gifts, as well, gifts that had been with them in life and were, over the course of eternity, strengthened, made more powerful.

Rogan, though, was only what he appeared to be—a warrior. A man who had known little else in life beyond the camaraderie of a battlefield and the company of others like himself. He'd served the last hereditary high king of Ireland, Brian Boru, and his last act on Earth had been to avenge his king's death. He valued loyalty. Honor.

And told himself that the vow he'd made so long ago was enough for him.

Then Alison Blair had walked into his home and short-circuited every nerve in his body. Just remembering her now brought back the flash of...*knowing* that had filled him with a simple touch. He'd dipped into her mind and felt her confusion. Felt her reaction to him and had had to fight to maintain the cold distance he preferred between himself and human-kind.

She was…*unexpected*. He'd thought only to be irritated with the intrusion of the Society. But with a single touch, that had changed. And he wasn't pleased with the knowledge.

Scowling, he cleared his mind and concentrated instead on the here and now. Thoughts of a woman he didn't want had no business on the hunt. He was needed. He did a job that few others could do, and this night he would track whatever demons thought to prey on his island.

While he moved through the darkness, becoming a part of the night itself, he thought of the seer's pre-diction. And again, despite his best intentions, of Alison Blair. He didn't want to think of her. He'd found and lost his Destined Mate centuries ago. There would be no other for him, and Rogan knew it was as well there wouldn't be. A hunter had no need for anything in his life but the next hunt. The next challenge. The next demon.

And as that thought rose up in his mind, he turned over the seer's warnings again. He had little patience with those who claimed to see the future. But since Alison's visit the night before, he'd done some re-search himself. True, he was more at home with a sword in his hand than he was sitting at a computer.

But he'd long ago learned that to move with a changing world, he had to first keep abreast of those changes.

He'd taught himself how to use the state-of-the-art computer system installed in his home, and his satellite Internet connection afforded him the luxury of researching anything he wished with the click of a button. And he'd found enough to make him wary, to make him consider using the Society's seer.

He seldom watched television and rarely read a newspaper, since the mortal world's interests had little to do with him. So it was with surprise that he found people were disappearing all over County Mayo. One or two at first, but in the past several weeks more and more were simply vanishing. The missing were generally young—in their twenties. And most of them were tourists, as though someone or some*thing* was endeavoring to keep the local population from becoming too suspicious.

Rogan moved out onto the road and stared up at the B and B where Alison Blair was staying. A farmhouse, the tidy white building fairly sparkled in the spare moonlight. Alongside the B and B was a stone-faced, thatched cottage used for self-catering vacationers. With the Lough behind him, Rogan stared at the B and B, shifting his gaze from one lamplit window to the next, focusing his mind and listening for the thoughts of those inside.

He heard children arguing, couples discussing a cathedral they'd toured that afternoon. The farmer who owned this land was laughing with his wife over something their eldest child had done, and a teenager was planning to slip out of his room and meet some friends.

And nowhere in that rush of thoughts was Alison Blair.

"Where in bloody hell is she?" Rogan muttered darkly, honing his concentration, searching all of those inside the house, looking for the American woman. With the link he had into the local system, he'd also combed through the guest registries all over the area until he'd found where she and her sister were staying while they were in Ireland.

He'd thought to talk to her again, to find out if that blasted seer had had anything more useful to say than the vague admonition she'd passed along. Damn the woman for not being where she should be.

Scowling off into the distance, he reached out with his senses, searching for some sign of her in the vicinity, but there was nothing. And irritation spiked inside him as he reached further, stretching his telepathic abilities out into the night even while he cursed her. She'd come all this way to give him the bloody message. Now that he actually wanted to speak with her, she was gone?

* * *

Aly walked up and down the sidewalk in front of the Sidhe pub, her gaze flicking constantly from side to side. Outside the square of light from the pub, the city streets were dark. Shops were closed and the few pedestrians on the sidewalks were scurrying, heads down, in the face of a sudden rain shower. Alison, though, tugged the hood of her jacket up and over her head and stood her ground. She wasn't sure what she was looking for exactly, but she knew she had to be here—where Casey had last been seen.

She strained to pick up any psychic signs of her sister, but there was nothing. All their lives, she and Casey had been able to link telepathically. Not that Aly was able to do this with anyone else, but she and her sister had always had such a close bond that they'd at least been able to touch each other's minds. But tonight there was nothing.

She'd almost gone to Rogan Butler to ask for help, but that impulse had disappeared fast. After all, he'd made it more than clear he hadn't wanted her around. And truth to tell, she was in no hurry to be that close to him again anyway. He was too much. Too handsome. Too powerful. Too overwhelming. And far too arrogant.

He hadn't wanted to listen to her about *business*. There was no way he'd care about her missing sister. She probably wouldn't even be allowed past his security guards again, so there was no point in trying to get in to see him anyway.

But that fact changed nothing. With or without help, she would find her sister. It had been just she and Casey for years. They were their only family, and they took care of each other. Wherever Casey was, she was counting on Aly to find her. So she would—even if she had to stand outside this pub and talk to everyone in Westport for the rest of her life. As a middle-aged couple darted past, headed for the pub, Aly hurried forward and intercepted them.

"Excuse me," she said.

"Why, you're American, aren't you?" The woman smiled a greeting as if she were expected to personally welcome all visitors to the city. "That's lovely."

"Thank you." Another woman hurried past them, and Aly dipped her head to avoid getting impaled by the points on her umbrella. Holding out a picture of her sister, Aly looked from the woman to her husband and back again. "I'm sorry to bother you, but my sister's missing and she was here last night. I'm trying to find her and—"

"Nice-looking girl," the man said, handing the picture back. "Haven't seen her, though."

"Sorry, love, I've not seen her either," the woman said, shaking her head solemnly. "Are you sure she's missing and not just off with a friend?"

"No," Aly said with a sigh of disappointment. It had been like this for two hours. Everyone she showed Casey's picture to had been kind and concerned but hadn't been able to help. Misery rose up inside her and did battle with fear. Fear was winning. "We only just arrived in Ireland yesterday, so she wouldn't have friends here to go off with."

"Come on, Bridget," the man said to his wife, yanking open the pub door to allow music, smoke and the scent of beer to escape.

His wife shooed him off, then waited for the door to close again before asking, "Have you spoken to the Garda?"

"Yes. They couldn't help me either."

She sighed in sympathy. "Terrible shame that is, love. So many young people going missing all of a sudden, you'd think the Garda could do something about it."

Aly swallowed hard, looked into the woman's eyes and fought down a growing sense of dread. "There've been a lot of missing people here lately?"

"Oh, yes. Mostly tourists, and Sean—that's my husband—he thinks nothin' of it. Says young people thrive on causing trouble."

"What do you think?" Aly asked, watching the elder woman shift her gaze around the well-lit square as if looking for something.

"I think," she said finally, softly, as if half afraid someone would hear her speak her own fears, "sometimes things happen that can't be explained." She shivered a little, shoved her hands into her coat pockets and offered a sad smile. "And I do hope you find your sister, love."

"Thank you." Aly whispered the words, staring down at the picture of Casey. But the woman had already slipped into the pub, leaving Aly alone on the sidewalk again.

Things that can't be explained...

That cold sense of dread coiled and tightened in the pit of Aly's belly, and she wished she could ease it. But how could she? She was in a position to know that what the woman had said was all too true. There *were* monsters out there, moving through the darkness, looking for prey. Demons from other dimensions, crowding into this world, taking what they could and destroying what they couldn't have.

Demons.

Lifting her head, Aly stared off into the shadows that bordered the river running alongside the town. From her post outside the pub, the rush of the water was more like a long undulating sigh, and she couldn't help feeling that it sounded lonely. Empty.

And she wondered about Casey. If she was safe. If she was afraid.

If she was alive.

Panic jolted through her, and it felt as though a tight fist had closed around her throat. Alive. Casey had to be alive. Of course she was. There was no reason to start the crazed imaginings of death and disaster. It was only that… "Oh, God. I never should have brought her here. Never should have let her go off alone. If anything's happened to her…"

She stopped, refusing to even finish that sentence. Her heart felt heavy, and her stomach was a churning mass of anxiety and sheer terror. She'd never felt more alone, more out of her element. Here on this tidy street corner, as everyone else in this lovely city went about their business, Aly was forced to admit the very real possibility that a demon might have her sister.

And if that were true…she'd *need* Rogan Butler to get Casey back.

Rogan shook his head, as if that motion alone could ease the frantic thoughts he was picking up from Alison Blair. He'd trained his telepathic abilities on her, homing in on the raging confusion in her mind, and followed her here to Westport. Now, he'd need only to locate her in the large seaport city.

He knew the town well. He'd watched it grow from its beginnings in the eighteenth century into a teeming city filled with, as far as he was concerned, too many mortals. But tonight he was interested in only one of the people wandering up and down these broad, familiar streets.

"Bloody woman." He bit the words off on an

oath. "If she'd stop letting her mind whirl in circles, she'd be easier to find."

There were no trace energy signals for him to follow. No sign of a demon as yet. There were only Alison's thoughts, a wild mix of pain and panic and sheer terror guiding him to her like the flash of a lighthouse across a churning sea. He felt an answering sense of urgency rise inside him and tried to tamp it down. She was nothing more to him than a clue to whatever was happening in his little corner of Ireland. And to defend those he was sworn to protect, he would use whatever information she could give him.

Beyond that, there was nothing.

Rogan used his Guardian abilities to obfuscate himself as he walked quickly down the wide riverfront street in Westport. He didn't have to be invisible, of course. But he'd found that a man of his size didn't pass through crowds unnoticed, and he'd rather keep his presence in the city quiet.

The river roared to his left, and from a corner pub music and laughter rose up in waves that filled the air. To his right, a drunk stumbled along the sidewalk, muttering to himself.

Rogan dismissed the man and continued on. His steps were long, measured, and the quiet that flowed with him streamed out around him in a wash of power. He was comfortable in the night, in the shadows where demons thrived and mortals feared to step. The adrenaline of the hunt pumped through his veins as he heard Alison's mind jumping from one thought to the next.

Alive. Casey's alive. I know it. But where? A demon? No. Rogan should be here. He's a Guardian. Maybe I should call the Society office in Dublin. And tell them what?

He stopped then, lifting his face to the wind, closing his eyes and focusing solely on Alison.

Where can I look? Where should I go next? I should find Rogan. No, he won't help. Casey needs me. What can I do? Oh, God, help me find her.

Her mind raged, calling to him, as if she were sensing his presence and guiding him to her. He felt her fear lying over her thoughts like a shroud, and he moved more quickly, hastening his steps as if in answer to her desperate call.

He homed in on her and loped across the wide street to round a corner. There, in the gold light spilling from the Sidhe pub, she stood. And swathed in a cloak of invisibility, he could watch her unseen. Study her features, drawn and tight with worry and fear. He looked into her blue eyes and read the signs of banked tears. He heard her thoughts and the wild, discordant prayers that she whispered as if they alone were enough to keep her safe.

And something inside him opened, welling, with a need he hadn't known in centuries. To comfort. To care for.

Rogan swiped one hand across his jaw, pulled in a breath and steadied himself. He wouldn't be drawn to this woman, because there could be nothing between them. He'd had his chance at an eternal love and had lost it when his Destined Mate had died at the hand of a demon.

A demon the seer had told him was gone.

Seers and women—both were more trouble than they were worth, and it would be best if he remembered that.

Before he could move to reveal himself to her, Alison's eyes suddenly widened. Her thoughts spun and unraveled like a spindle of thread dropped to roll on the ground. She ran past him, and as she did, he caught the uppermost thought in her mind.

Demon.

Whirling around, he chased after her and caught her in just a step or two, his big hand coming down on her shoulder and pulling her to a stop.

She screamed.

"Hush now," he ordered in a tight, cold voice.

"Rogan?" She looked around wildly, her eyes darting from one side to the other, trying to find him and not succeeding. "Where are you?"

Cursing viciously, he dropped the energy cloak masking his presence, and she was staring up at him in stunned surprise. "Sorry. Forgot I was invisible."

She choked out a harsh laugh that sounded more like a taut sob than anything else and instantly clapped one hand across her mouth. "Now there's something you don't hear every day. Where did you come from? How did you find me?"

"I followed your thoughts."

"God, that's right. You can read minds."

"And yours is a jumble at the moment, if you don't mind my sayin' so," he told her, releasing her almost reluctantly. "Where were you runnin' off to just then? And why were you thinkin' *'demon'*?"

"Because I saw—" She half turned to point at the river walk. "Out there. It was just for a second. But I'm sure I saw a trace energy. It was almost purple, with some red, and it was gone very quickly. But I know I saw it."

Stunned, he simply stared at her for a long moment. "You can read demon energy?"

"A bit." She backed away from him, heading for the river. "All Society members are a bit psychic, some more than others. And I *know* what I saw."

"I believe you." And he did. He could see the truth in her eyes, hear it in her voice. He could practically feel the feverish intent to chase down a demon humming around her like an aura of emotion. "But you're not to be chasing demons, Alison Blair. What did you think you'd do with it once you'd caught it?"

"I—" She stopped, took a breath and then shoved the hood off her face. A few drops of rain landed on her cheeks and glistened in the lamplight like tears. "I don't know. I only know I have to follow it. My sister. Casey."

He already knew what was driving her. Hadn't he been latched on to her mind for the past half hour or more? "I know. She's gone."

She staggered as if his words had carried a physical punch. Her bottom lip quavered, but she bit down on it. "I don't know what happened to her. She was here at this pub last night. I spoke to a waitress who saw her leave. Alone. But after that there's just nothing…"

Alison turned her head to look through the pub's window at the laughing, dancing people inside, and she was so wistful, so lost, she made his heart hurt. Something it hadn't done in a very long time.

Bristling at the very notion, Rogan straightened to his full height and looked down at her. "What makes you think a demon has her?"

"What else could have happened? She isn't at the hospitals. Hasn't been arrested. She doesn't know anyone here, so she's not staying with a friend." She shook her head slowly and looked away from him, staring off into the shadows as if expecting to find her sister there waiting for her. "She's vanished, Rogan, and no one's seen her. Anywhere." She wiped away the stray raindrops from her cheeks with the back of her hand.

She blew out a breath and sucked in another. "There are others missing, too. Lots of them.

Tourists are disappearing, and I believe it's got something to do with the seer's warning. There is something rising here and I think it's got Casey." She stepped up close to him, tilted her head back and met his gaze with a steadiness he admired. "I've got to get her back. And you've got to help me."

Behind them the pub door opened and noise and smoke rolled out around them. A couple, linked arm in arm, ran from the pub and down the sidewalk, laughing. Rogan, though, paid them no attention.

Grabbing Alison's arm, he ignored the instantaneous burn that erupted between them and dragged her farther from the lights, deeper into the shadows. When he was sure they were alone, he let her go and said, "You've no business following a demon." When she started to argue with him, he cut her off neatly and kept talking, his voice going deeper, more rough with every word. "I've seen this before, you know. Society members spend so much time studying Guardians that they begin to believe they, too, are capable of battling the demons. It's a false confidence, and all it causes is more death. If you go after a demon, you'll get yourself killed."

She stepped back from him, and despite the darkness, the determined gleam in her eyes shone at him. He actually itched to touch her again. A humming sense of intensity built inside him, roaring like a fire just catching the tinder. He hadn't felt that particular warmth in more years than he cared to count and wasn't at all grateful to be feeling it now.

"I'm not an idiot. I wouldn't try to capture a demon. But I *can* follow one."

"To what end?"

"Finding my sister, of course. What else?"

"You've no idea if she's being held by a demon or not."

"I'm out of options, Rogan," she muttered, turning her gaze from him, back to the shadows that edged the riverside. A moment later Alison lifted one hand and pointed. "There! There it is again. Do you see it?"

"Aye. I see it." It amazed him to know that *she* could see that faint wash of pale purple and red twisting in the night wind. But clearly she could. There was more to Alison Blair than he might have thought. And the danger of that was all too clear to him.

If he didn't step in, keep her from following whatever demon was haunting the shadows of Westport, Alison would do it herself.

She was willing to risk her life to find her sister.

And as a Guardian, he was duty bound to protect her.

Chapter 4

Alison wasn't about to waste precious seconds as they ticked inexorably past. She simply set off in the direction she'd seen the demon's energy signal and expected Rogan to follow her. She wasn't disappointed.

For a huge man, he moved so quietly he might as well have been invisible again. And hadn't *that* been a surprise and a half! To feel unseen hands grab her...to hear that deep, musical voice telling her to be quiet...and to see not a soul.

Of course, she knew about the Guardians' ability to obfuscate themselves, but she'd never really seen that ability in action. The way she'd jumped and yelped had really been professional. Oh, she was not at all prepared to be a field operative. And the thought of following a demon to find Casey absolutely terrified her. But she had no choice in this. So when Rogan grabbed her again, none too gently, she ignored the arc of something hot and delicious jolting through her system and turned to face him, fire in her eyes.

The furious expression on his face made her almost wish he'd go invisible again. "Come on. If we don't follow what's left of that energy signature, we'll lose the demon."

"*We'll* do nothing of the kind," he said and gave her arm another squeeze before releasing her. "You're tracking no demons while I'm here."

"You can't stop me."

"I can, yes. Don't push me on this, Alison Blair. I've no use for the Society and even less use for a woman on a hunt."

"You really are a caveman, aren't you?"

He seemed to swell in indignation. His broad chest widening, his square jaw tight, his green eyes flashing with a banked fury. "I'm a Guardian, in case you've forgotten. This is *my* job, not yours."

"And Casey is *my* sister, not yours." She wouldn't back down. Couldn't. He'd just said it himself. Casey was no more than a job to him. He wasn't involved in this. Not really. He didn't *care* as she did.

The rush of the nearby river blended with the sigh of the wind and the patter of the rain falling down around them in fat, lazy drops.

"You've a car, don't you?" he demanded.

"Yes."

"Then get in it and go back to your B and B. If I find anything, I'll let you know."

Her jaw dropped. Surely he didn't actually expect that to happen. "I can't go back without Casey."

"You can and you will. Now."

That last word was emphasized, and he stared her down as if daring her to contradict him. She would have, too. But in a small, still-rational corner of her mind, her own voice whispered that she was wasting time—that Rogan Butler was a legendary Guardian, that if anyone could find Casey, it would be *he*. But he needed her along. She knew Casey. He didn't. Her younger sister would be terrified by the huge warrior if Aly wasn't along to reassure her.

Deliberately, she took another step toward the river. "I'll go when I see you're on the demon's trail. When I know you've got some clue as to where Casey is."

Muttering under his breath, he stalked past her, the sound of his movement lost in the sigh of the river. The rush of Gaelic pouring from him sounded both musical and enraged. When he finally spoke in English again, it was short and sweet. "Stay behind me. And the hell out of my way."

"Charming," she murmured, but did as he said, taking two or three steps for every one of his. He moved along the river walk, his gaze darting from side to side, checking every shadow, searching every corner he passed. Casey, too, kept her gaze alert, hoping to see another swirl of color, some trace of the demon that had been moving through here only moments ago.

But there seemed to be nothing, only the quiet rush of the river and the dark that seemed to spill along the streets. The moon was hidden now beneath a bank of clouds still spitting rain, and the blend of fiddle and drum from the pub seemed distant and dreamlike.

Her breath came in short, hard gasps as she struggled to keep up with the Guardian, who clearly didn't care if she fell behind. Maybe he was going so quickly on purpose. To prove to her that she couldn't keep up. That she had no business being on a hunt.

Aly didn't know. Didn't care. Her gaze locked on Rogan's broad back, she ignored her surroundings. Her mind was too filled with pictures of her sister. Images of Casey in danger. Hurt. Scared. Alone.

She felt only the barest brush of heat on the back of her neck an instant before something grabbed her. Fear exploded inside her as she took one quick gasp of air. Long, thick fingers curled around the base of her throat, cutting off another breath and burning into her skin as if each of those fingers was a living flame.

Aly stumbled, then was brought up hard and flush against the body of her captor, standing behind her.

"Lovely." A voice sighed out around her, sneaking into her bones, sliding through her blood. Both hot and cold seemed to wash over her as she stared ahead of her into the darkness, straining to see Rogan.

Fear was alive and well and crouched in the pit of her stomach. The being behind her lifted her off the ground until she struggled to keep her toes on the cobbled street beneath her. Anything to maintain the narrow passage of air struggling to fill her lungs. She yanked at the hand at her throat, but it was like trying to pull a steel bar off a blocked door. Power hummed around her, and that voice came again, close, as her captor dipped its head to her ear.

"You follow me. You and the Guardian. Is he training you? Are you a sweet young thing only learning to fight us?"

Demon.

She shook her head wildly and gasped as the demon's fingers tightened on her throat like a well-tied noose. Where was Rogan? He hadn't gotten that far ahead of her. What kind of Guardian was it who would leave her to be killed? Hadn't he noticed the demon? Hadn't he sensed its presence?

Fingers on her throat tightened further, and small black-and-white dots danced in her vision.

"Release her."

The demon holding her spun around so awkwardly that Aly lost her tenuous balance and hung limply in the demon's clutches. Deliberately, she lifted both hands to the viselike grip on her throat, taking her weight up a bit so she could fight for the air she needed so desperately.

Through narrowed eyes, she stared at Rogan, standing only a few feet from her. His black hair lifted in the wind, and his green eyes flashed a warning so bright it was easy to read even in the darkness.

"I think not," the demon cooed and bent its head to sniff at Aly's throat. She shuddered as its cold, rough skin scraped along her jaw, her neck.

Rogan's big hand fisted on the hilt of the sword he held, and his body seemed to vibrate with menace. "You think to save yourself by hiding behind a woman, then?"

The demon laughed softly, and somehow that made it even worse. Aly closed her eyes, and a single tear squeezed out from behind her lids and traced down along her cheek. Her grip on the demon's hand was fading as her strength slid away.

"I don't hide, Guardian." The demon stroked one hand down the line of her body and with the last of her strength, Aly tried to move away from that touch. "I take what I find and I use it. I found her. She's mine."

"As well you know, not a thing on this plane of existence is yours, demon. So let's be at it and leave the woman."

A snarl and snap of teeth hissed into the night as the demon spat at Rogan. "I'll leave her when I'm done with her and not before. If you go now, Guardian, I might let her live. After."

The river rushed past her on her right. From a distance, Aly heard the faint beat of music. A cold wind ruffled her hair and made her eyes tear as she opened them to look helplessly at Rogan. She was dying. She felt her sluggish heart slow. Felt her own end coming and knew there was nothing she could do about it. But then she looked into Rogan's eyes.

When I go for him, drop to the ground and stay there.

His words rumbled through her mind, but that wasn't possible. She was psychic, not telepathic. But maybe she was hallucinating. Maybe she was hearing what she wanted to hear. She was dying. She knew it.

An instant later Rogan howled, his voice rising into a bellowing shriek of justice as he charged the demon holding Aly so tightly. The demon, startled, loosened its grip for a second, and with her last ounce of energy, Aly pulled free, dropped to the ground and stayed there. Her lungs greedily sucked in air, the blurriness of her vision cleared and the pounding in her head eased back into just a memory of the pain she'd had moments before.

And as she lay there, on the cold, wet sidewalk, the sounds of battle over and around her clashed like thunder. The demon cried out, Rogan's sword sang as it slashed through the air and Aly turned her face to see. Rogan's features were cold and tight, but he moved with a grace and blinding speed that left her awed. His reputation was well deserved. He fought like a man possessed, but his movements were almost a dance of destruction.

A high-pitched shriek of pain sliced neatly through the blackness, and a heavy thud hit the ground near her. Instinctively, Aly tried to back away from the fallen demon. It wasn't dead—she knew demons were almost impossible to kill in this dimension—but its eyes were closed and blood ran black down the side of its face.

Rogan plucked her off the ground a heartbeat later, as if she weighed no more than a child. His easy strength was as impressive as the rest of him. "Are you well?"

"Yeah," she said, nodding and shaking and trying to keep from falling back to the ground in a shuddering heap. "I'm fine. My throat hurts," she added, lifting one hand to the base of her throat where she could still feel the imprint of the demon's fingers on her skin.

"Turn to me."

"What?"

He took her face in one big palm and turned her until he could see her throat. Frowning, he said, "Bastard burned you. You'll have to put something on that."

On the ground at their feet, the demon moved, trying to ease off into the shadows while the Guardian was distracted. It didn't work. Rogan slammed his sword through the demon's body and straight through the sidewalk. The demon wailed again but was held fast, like a butterfly on a straight pin to a board.

"Oh, God…" Aly swallowed hard, ran her fingers over the rough flesh at the base of her throat and then looked away from the demon. Yes, it had tried to kill her. Yes, it was a demon. But seeing it impaled on a sword was something she didn't enjoy.

"Go now," Rogan was saying and this time his voice, though still a dark murmur, was gentler. "Back to the B and B. I'll take this one back to its portal and search for your sister."

"I should—"

"—go," he finished for her.

And truth to tell, Aly knew he was right. She hadn't been any help. Rogan would no doubt be able to find more information if she wasn't trailing along, slowing him down. It cost her, but a moment later she nodded and said, "Fine. I'll go. But I expect to hear from you by the end of the night."

His mouth flattened into a tight, grim slash as he shook his head. And when he spoke, the gentleness was gone, replaced by that steely sound of arrogance she'd already come to know so well. "I knew having the Society poking into things was only going to bollix things up."

The demon whimpered and Rogan gave it a kick. "Have some pride, demon."

It snarled and Aly skipped back a pace. She was in no shape for another round of demon fighting. Although you could hardly call being slowly strangled *fighting*. And now that she was recovering, she was also able to feel a little ashamed of how badly she'd handled herself.

Every Society member was trained in hand-to-hand combat on the off chance that he or she might one day confront a demon. And the day she *did* get that confrontation? What had she done? She'd hung like a puppet from the demon's hand, and if it hadn't been for Rogan, she'd be dead now and Casey would have no one to look for her.

"Where's your car, Alison Blair?"

"Parked on James Street."

He scowled, lifted his head and scented the ever-present Irish wind. "I sense nothing but this demon here. Though it may be its presence is masking another."

"I'll be fine."

"Aye, you will, as I'll be taking you to your car." He reached into the inside of his long, black coat, pulled something from a pocket and whipped it out into the wind. A net, as fine as spider webbing, briefly glinted a shining silver in the dim light.

The net dropped over the demon, still twisting against the blade holding it in place, and a heartbeat later the demon, the sword and the net disappeared from view.

"Wow."

"I've sealed it in a bubble. No passing human will stumble across it now, and it won't be escaping the net."

Aly knew about the net but again had never seen one close up. Made of microscopic silver links, the net was strong enough to hold any demon and prevent escape. Every Guardian carried one because they were forced to drag demons to portals, returning them to the dimensions they'd left to infiltrate our world.

Aly turned for another look as Rogan took her arm and hurried her down the street toward her car, but the sidewalk was empty. No sign of the demon, the sword or the Guardian's presence. It was as if none of this had happened at all. The only thing left to remind her of her first encounter with a demon was the burning sensation at the base of her throat.

"How did you know to fall when I attacked the demon?" Rogan asked, his voice carrying a hint of false innocence.

"I heard you."

He blew out a breath and muttered what she guessed was a curse in Gaelic. She guessed it sounded much better in the old Irish language than it would have in English.

"At least, I think I heard you," Aly said, shaking her head as if the memory wasn't quite clear and a little jostling might firm things up. "Maybe not. Maybe it was just looking at your face and being able to tell what you were about to do."

"Aye. That was probably it."

"That's my car."

He dragged her toward it, his hand on her arm more that of a jailer than a concerned Guardian. When he released her, she couldn't help missing the heat of his touch, though she wouldn't admit that even to herself.

"Get in it, then. Go back to your inn. Wait there."

"You'll find Casey?" Aly wouldn't be brushed off. Not by him. Not by a demon. Casey was all she had, and she wasn't going to risk losing her.

"If she's there to be found, I'll find her. Now for the love of God, woman, go away."

She climbed into her car and sat there in the silence, her gaze trained on Rogan Butler as he strode away. She watched until he disappeared into the shadows.

* * *

Rage moved with Rogan as he entered his home. The night was nearly over, and his body was still primed for battle. The demon that had grabbed Alison hadn't been enough of a challenge for him, but the second one he'd found, down by the harbor, had proven to be a formidable opponent.

He rubbed his left arm with his right hand and felt the still-closing wound the demon had given him with a swipe of its claws. Guardians healed quickly, and he knew that by the next night, all but a faint reminder of that injury would be gone. Yet, he rubbed the spot on his upper arm now, remembering.

"You seek the girl, Guardian," the demon *screamed at him with a taunting laughter that bordered on hysteria. "But she's gone from you."*

"Talk now and tell me what I need to know," *Rogan said, giving the demon a shake that rattled its eyes in their sockets, "or you go back to your hell with the mark of my blade in your chest."*

The demon cringed, knowing that the sword wouldn't kill it, only cause extreme agony. Yet it held its secrets, refusing to speak no matter the torment Rogan put it through. At last, frustrated and enraged, Rogan opened the portal and shoved the demon through.

Now here, in the quiet of his home, he knew he would have to tell Alison Blair that she'd been right.

A demon was holding her sister, and they had no idea which demon it was. Or which dimension to look in for her.

He dropped his coat, the pockets filled with knives, throwing stars and the Guardian net, across the first chair he passed and walked straight to the bar across the room. He bent down, opened the small refrigerator and pulled out a Guinness. Twisting off the top and tossing it onto the bar, he turned, already taking a long drink.

Only to nearly spew the liquid out when he spotted Alison asleep in a chair. While unresolved fury battered his insides, he studied her in the lamplight. She'd fallen asleep with a book open on her lap and her head pillowed against one of the wings of the chair. She wore faded blue jeans and a soft-looking white sweater that hugged her body and rose high enough on her neck to hide the burns the demon had left her with. Her legs were curled up under her, and her pale, long blond hair fell down across her shoulders to lie over her breasts.

His body went hard as steel as he felt the now-too-familiar hum of need pulsing through him. He didn't want this. Didn't want a connection to a woman who could only mean trouble for him in the long run. But did he have a choice? She was here. Despite his telling her to go to the inn, she'd come here. To wait for him. And though a part of him appreciated her stubbornness, that didn't mean he could allow her to stay.

The ache in his shoulder faded away as he remembered the flash of heat that arced between them when he touched her. And there was more. There was the fact that she'd *heard* the telepathic order he'd issued when that demon first laid hands on her.

He hadn't been sure she would but had thought it worth a try. The fact that she *had* heard him only filled him with more conflicted feelings than he wanted. A Destined Mate would be able to hear his thoughts. But she'd said herself she was psychic. Society members all had varying levels of psychic ability. Perhaps it was no more than that.

It *had* to be no more than that. All Guardians were given the promise of a Destined Mate, one who was meant for them. One who, if found, would bond with the Guardian and strengthen their powers. Connect at a soul-deep level.

For centuries, Rogan thought as he stared down at her, thoughtfully sipping his beer, he'd doubted the veracity of the Mate legend. Then, he'd met his. Sinead O'Donnel. A short, curvy woman with long black hair, bright blue eyes and the devil's own temper.

But she died.

So many years ago now. He could, at times, convince himself that he'd only imagined the flash of heat between them. The *need* that had brought him to his knees. The aching ferocity of the touch of her mouth to his.

His body went, if possible, even harder. Every inch of him groaned with a desire that Rogan refused to recognize. He was a warrior. Battle trained. Strong enough to outlast eons of skirmishes and conflict. He would *not* surrender to the rush of lust clamoring to be turned loose.

"Alison Blair." He said her name in a low-throated shout that had her jerking into awareness and blinking wide blue eyes at him.

"You're back."

"I am, yes," he said, taking another pull of the icy, black beer, hoping the cold would tamp the fires raging within. "My question to you is, what the bloody hell are you doing here?"

She pushed herself up from the chair, setting the book down on the nearby table. Running one hand through her hair, she shoved it back from her face and blinked wildly in an attempt to rid herself of the befuddlement of sleep. "I couldn't just go back to the B and B and pretend everything was fine. I had to be here when you got back with Casey."

She looked around the room, then back at him. "But you don't have her, do you?"

His back teeth ground together at the not-too-subtle reminder that he'd failed. Failure was not something Rogan Butler was familiar with. He did his job, carried out his duty and, by God, beat the demon horde back at every turn. Until tonight, damn it all to hell. "I do not. And you don't belong here."

She lifted her chin and glared at him. "Of course I belong here. And I'm not leaving. I checked out of the inn. Brought mine and Casey's things here. Your housekeeper, Maggie, was very helpful. Even *she* agreed that it makes more sense for me to be here. Close by."

He laughed shortly, walked back to the bar and set the now-empty beer bottle down on top of it. Later, he'd be having a little chat with Maggie Riordan. The fiftyish woman had been running his household for nearly thirty years though, and he'd never won a bloody argument with her. He had no doubt she'd find a way to make him feel small and selfish for trying to deny Alison Blair a room in a house with more than ample space for guests.

But there were reasons, damned good reasons, for not having Alison under his roof. Reasons that didn't concern Maggie or any other bloody soul but himself.

"It's not like we're strangers, Rogan. I've read all about you," she reminded him. "And I know about the Guardians, so there's no worries there about secrets being spilled." She paused to yawn, then shook her head fiercely and said, "I have to be here. I have to help you find my sister."

He heard the determination in her voice and saw the fatigue in her eyes. She was a woman who wouldn't be put off with platitudes and promises. She was the type who would stick her bloody nose into his business until she was sure she'd discovered all she needed to know.

Inside him, his guts twisted in a weird tangle of wants and needs. Just looking at her made his body ache. Her presence here, in his home, would be a constant reminder of what he'd lost so long ago. But he couldn't deny the lush, thick attraction between them, either. And he was not a man used to ignoring sexual needs.

"I can help," she insisted, unaware of the track his mind was taking. "I have the resources of the Society behind me."

"I've no need of you for that," he told her, not wanting to admit just what he *might* need her for. Damned if the woman didn't look as though she'd just had a good tumble.

Her hair, long and thick and shining gold in the lamplight, tempted him. He wanted to thread his fingers through the mass, drag her head to his and cover her mouth with his own. Maybe a kiss would be enough to ease the torment. Maybe then he'd be able to draw a bloody breath.

And maybe not.

Ignoring the desire shaking him, he said, "The Society is there to serve the Guardians. They'll answer my questions as well as you could. Should I have any."

She chewed at her bottom lip, and he watched the motion, feeling an answering tug deep inside him. His damned body was betraying him as he stood there. He felt thick and hard and ready, and she stood there like a damned innocent, unaware of what she did to him simply by filling the room with her scent.

"I can research for you."

"I've no need of that."

"I can help you on the hunt."

He laughed aloud now, grateful for the respite. "Aye, you were a big help tonight, distracting that demon by strangling so."

"It caught me off guard."

"Bloody woman," he muttered, crossing the room to grab her upper arms and drag her close. Close enough that her beguiling scent filled his head, his heart, his veins. He was surrounded by her, and the heat pooling between them threatened to boil. Drawing her up to her toes, he pushed his face into hers and said, "That's what demons do, catch you off guard. Then they kill."

"I'm not an idiot," she argued, matching him glare for glare even as her breath quickened along with his. Even as the lightninglike arc of something hot and incredible danced back and forth in the space between them. "I wasn't ready tonight, I admit that. Fine. Happy? But arguing with you and being worried just shattered my concentration. I'll do better next time. You'll see. I know what to do. I know how to defend myself. I won't get in your way, but I won't leave either. Not until we find Casey and bring her back."

"You've a death wish, is that it?"

"No," she said, and her blue eyes shone into his, heat flashing in their depths until Rogan felt himself burning up inside. "And I'm not looking for a red-hot affair with a crabby-ass Guardian either, so you can just quit making those little lightning special effects, if you don't mind."

He shook his head, and his fingers curled harder into her arms, as if he could somehow mitigate the wildness erupting inside by holding her even tighter. "I'm not the one creating those feelings. And if I'd any control over them at all, they wouldn't be happening. That's something neither of us can prevent. But just so you know, I'm no more interested than you are."

Lies, he thought grimly, all lies. He was too damn interested. Not in a Mate, God knew. But he'd be lying again if he didn't at least admit to himself that he'd like to toss her across his bed and—

"Good," she said, pushing at the immovable wall of his chest with both hands. "Because if that feeling's what I think it is, I'm so not interested. I'm no one's Destined Mate, Rogan. I've got a life I like just the way it is, and I'm going back to it as soon as we find Casey."

He inhaled sharply, deeply, ordering his mind to

calm, his blood to cool. He fought the sensations blistering the air between himself and the woman who had so complicated his life. Just because those sensations existed was not to say they had to act on them.

"Fine, then," he said and let her go so abruptly she staggered back a step or two, trying to find her balance.

His palms hummed, his fingers itched to touch her again and his cock felt as though it were hard as a diamond. The ache of need washed over him, but it was a personal agony he'd simply have to learn to live with.

At least until he could get Alison Blair out of his life and out of his country. He wouldn't be able to relax his guard until there was an ocean separating them.

"We'll work together as long as you do as I say," he warned, lifting one finger and pointing it at her meaningfully. "And the moment we've found your sister, you leave Ireland and never come back."

Chapter 5

"Deal," she said and held out one hand to him.

Rogan looked at her small hand and noted how fragile it seemed. She stood before him with a warrior's gleam in her shining blue eyes, but in reality she was small and defenseless in his world. Then he remembered how she had looked, in the grip of the demon that had grabbed her by the throat, and his insides fisted into tightly coiled bands of steel.

In his memory he saw again that despite her fear she'd kept her senses. Moved when he wanted her to move, stayed down when he needed her to keep out of the way. And in spite of what she'd gone through, she hadn't run for safety to the inn—she'd come here, to him, insisting on being a part of the hunt for the demon. She was outmatched in strength, cunning and sheer meanness, but she wouldn't be excluded, and a part of him admired her courage.

Even while another part of him wished that for both their sakes she had avoided him as she should have.

She was waiting, her hand still out in a gesture of peace—temporary camaraderie. He took her hand gently in his, folding his much larger fingers around hers, and as he did, he felt that buzzing sensation build up between them again. It was as if each of them separately was a live electrical wire and when brought together, the power that leaped into life was twice their individual power.

And while he admitted that the feeling between them was strong, he also knew he would ignore what those feelings might mean for as long as he could. When he finally released her, she swallowed hard and winced.

"Are you injured?"

Instinctively, she lifted one hand to the base of her throat, covered by the high, white neck of her sweater. "It's fine. Really."

"You're a terrible liar." Reaching out, he tucked his fingers in the neck of the sweater and pulled the soft fabric away from her skin. Her raw, reddened flesh made him hiss in a breath. With everything else going on, he'd forgotten about the burn she'd suffered earlier in the night. Shifting his gaze to hers, he saw pain glittering in her eyes, and he wondered why he hadn't noticed it before. Then he knew. He hadn't seen it because he hadn't *wanted* to see it. Because knowing she'd been injured— while under his protection—was something he couldn't tolerate.

"Come with me." He took her hand, accepting the sizzle and buzz that erupted at that simple touch, and nearly dragged her from the room. Her steps sounded loud in the room as she hustled to keep up with his much longer strides, but he didn't slow down any. Annoyance pushed at him, feeding his impatience. He turned right at the foyer and pulled her up the staircase behind him.

From the kitchen came the scent of pot roast cooking, and that reminded him that he had to have a chat with Maggie, but first things first.

The dark red carpet runner up the center of the stairs muffled their steps until they sounded more like heartbeats than footfalls. Wall sconces threw soft halos of light along the stairs, illuminating the paintings in elaborately carved frames that he'd collected over the long years of his life. Rogan paid them no attention at all. Instead, he hit the second-floor landing and turned right again, headed for his own room at the end of the wide hall.

"You don't have to run, you know."

"I'm not running."

"Then slow down," she said, trying to tug her hand free of his.

He only tightened his grip. "The demon burns must be treated."

"You told me to put stuff on it. I did. I'm fine."

"You'll not lie to me again. Ever."

"I'm not lying," she argued and tried again to pull free of him, but his strength made that attempt, and any others like it, a futile one. "I put some salve on the burns as soon as I got here. They'll heal."

He paused at the closed door to his room, looked back at her over his shoulder and pierced her gaze with his own. "The burn of a demon won't heal with your puny human medicines."

"Puny?" She laughed in spite of the situation.

"Aye. Puny." He almost smiled, felt a twist of his lips coming and deliberately squashed the impulse. "Come on, then. In here."

Alison stepped into his room and stopped dead on the threshold. She hadn't been really sure what to expect. Rogan was, after all, one of the oldest Guardians. But this definitely wasn't it.

The room was…lush. That was the only word that even came close to describing it. Heavy, blood-red drapes hung at the windows, open now to the night. A blistering fire crackled in a stone fireplace, sending waves of warmth into the cavernous room.

A bed wide enough for six people to sleep comfortably was against the far wall, and the high mattress was covered with a duvet the same shade of red as the drapes. Mountains of pillows were stacked against the dark wood headboard that stood at least four feet tall. The carvings on the board were muted in the dim light, and Alison had the urge to go over to inspect it, to see what kind of images most appealed to a warrior such as Rogan Butler. But she didn't get the chance.

He turned, lifted her off her feet, carried her across the room and plopped her down on the end of the bed. The mattress beneath her was soft and incredibly welcoming. She hadn't even noticed until that moment just how tired she was. But now, all she wanted to do was lie down, close her eyes and lose herself in the softness beneath her.

"Wait there," he said, giving her a look that dared her to move an inch.

While he stalked across the room and through an open doorway that led, no doubt, to a bathroom, she studied the rest of his bedroom. Four tall posts jutted up from the corners of the bed, the dark wood, twisted into spirals, gleamed from years of careful polishing. A wide dresser stood along one wall, and directly opposite the bed, a wide-screen TV hung on the far wall.

Strangely enough, the sight of the television calmed her down a little as she listened to drawers being yanked open and slammed shut. An ancient warrior he might be, but clearly Rogan Butler was male enough to want the most expensive toys he could find. Shelves on either side of the television held books and DVDs.

Glancing at the open door to the bathroom to make sure he wasn't watching, she scooted off the edge of the bed and walked across the room to the shelves. The books were classics, leather-bound volumes of fiction and poetry with a few paperback novels thrown in to spice things up…the DVDs consisted of a collection of horror movies. Turning her head, she squinted at the titles and found a few classics there, as well. *Dracula, Friday the 13th, Halloween…*

"You watch a lot of movies, do you?" she called out.

Scowling, he came out of the bathroom, carrying gauze, tape and a small jar filled with a brown substance. Immediately, he narrowed his eyes on her. "I told you to stay put."

"And perhaps you've noticed I don't take orders very well."

"We struck a bargain. You will do as I tell you—"

"About demons, sure." Aly met his glare and stood her ground. She had to make her point here or be lost. She wanted to be a partner in the search for Casey, and if she didn't put her foot down from the start, that wouldn't happen. "But you can't tell me sit and stay. I'm not an Irish setter."

"More's the pity," he mumbled and shifted his supplies to one hand as he took her arm with the other and dragged her back to the bed. "Sit. Stay."

She actually smiled. "Was that humor?"

"Unlikely. I'm not in the least amused at the moment."

She planted her hands on the mattress and hopped up to the edge of the bed. Her legs swung at least a foot off the floor as she watched him lay out the supplies he'd gathered. "So, you watch a lot of movies?"

"Some."

"Horror flicks."

He lifted one massive shoulder in a shrug. "They relax me."

Now she did laugh. "Nobody watches scary movies to relax and— *What* is that stuff?"

He'd unscrewed the lid of the jar and a hideous odor wafted free of it. Her nose wrinkled and she tried to breathe through her mouth to cut down on the smell. It didn't work.

"You'll have to take off the sweater."

She scooted back from him. "Oh, I don't think so."

He sighed, dipped a finger into the brown substance and held it out to her. It gleamed a dark, honey-brown in the light and looked as if it were trying to ooze off his hand under its own power.

"That's just gross."

"It will heal the burn, but it will also ruin your sweater. So off with it."

She looked from him to the ooze and back again. "I think I'd rather have the burn. Honest. It feels better already."

Rogan drew in a long breath, and Aly watched his chest swell to massive proportions. The man was a giant, and she had one quick moment to wonder what he must have been like back in his own time. Her imagination quickly filled in the blanks for her—she saw him as he must have been, standing in the middle of a battlefield, a giant among smaller men, swinging his sword over his head and howling in fury.

Just thinking about it made her heart skip a little, but when she shook her head to clear it, he was still standing there, waiting.

"You'll do as I say, or you'll be taken back to the B and B this night."

He'd do it, too. He was anxious to be rid of her anyway and would love to grab hold of a good excuse. Well, she wasn't going to give him one. "Fine. Turn around."

She'd caught him off guard. His eyes widened in surprise, but a second later he did as she asked and turned his back to her. Quickly, Aly slipped out of the sweater, then held it to her chest. The fire in the hearth crackled and sent dancing shadows out into the room, but the air was still cool enough to raise goose bumps on her skin.

"Okay, you can turn around again."

She was covered. Not only by her bra but by the sweater she was clutching in front of her. So why did his gaze make her feel as if she were naked and tied to an altar stone? He seemed to see right through her clothing, searing her skin with a look hot enough to boil her blood. A moment ticked past, and then another, while he simply stared at her and Aly pulled in one long, shaky breath. "Um," she said, unable to bear the strained silence another minute, "so what's in that stuff? It looks and, hey, smells gross."

Her voice shook him out of whatever thoughts had brought him to a standstill. Grimacing tightly, he said, "It's an old recipe. Magically enhanced. A wizard makes it for me."

"A wizard?"

"Turn your head. Aye, a wizard."

She tipped her head back to allow him access to the burned skin at the base of her neck, and she had a wild thought that she looked like a woman on the cover of a romance novel. Head back, eyes closed, fire flickering in the background as an ancient warrior loomed close.

Of course, no self-respecting heroine would be clutching her sweater in front of her like a modern-day chastity shield or something. To derail that train of thought, she started talking again.

"Which wizard? I mean, I've read of a few who work with the Guardians and—" His fingers touched her skin, smoothing that brown goo on her burn, and instantly she felt both soothed and scalded.

Yes, the substance took the pain from the demon's mark—like a miracle of sorts—but Rogan's touch built an entirely different kind of fire. The kind that didn't ache, only burned. It felt as though his touch were slipping beneath her skin, to stroke the very essence of her.

The sizzle and punch of the connection humming between them arced into the room, linking them, whether they wanted it or not. Her eyes flew open and she stared up at him. His features were in partial shadow, with the soft light caressing his hard face, making him look—not soft, by any means, but more…approachable. And that probably wasn't a good thing.

"Rogan—"

"It's helping. Already begun to heal," he whispered, and his voice was thick, deep enough to reverberate through her bones, her soul.

Aly couldn't tear her gaze from him. His eyes flashed with light. His stern mouth was firmed into a grim line, and the muscle in his jaw twitched as he silently fought for the control she'd already lost. She knew he felt what she did. Knew there was more going on here than she wanted. And still she yearned to feel his hands not just on her neck but also on her body.

She imagined what it would be like, to lie beneath him, to feel his hard body covering hers, sliding into hers. She inhaled sharply, instinctively arching toward him, and she heard him hiss in a breath just before he stepped back.

Wiping the goo from his hand with a towel he'd brought with him, Rogan then reached for a gauze pad and the medical tape. Quickly he finished dressing the burn on her throat, then looked down at her. "You'll be fine by morning."

"Thanks," she whispered, still shaken by the force of her thoughts, the images provided by her mind. He was telepathic. Had he read her? Had he seen what she'd been thinking, wondering about? Had he wanted to…

"Aye," he muttered thickly, pushing one big hand through his hair with impatience. "I did and I do." He snapped her a hard look. "But I won't."

Well, that answered her questions. He had seen her thoughts. Had shared her wants. And he was going to ignore them. "Probably best," she said softly, still holding that sweater to her chest.

"It is," he agreed. "We've neither one of us a desire to make our association more than it is. Best to leave things as they lie."

"Right." She nodded, still staring at him, wondering what he was thinking now. If he was burning up on the inside, as she was. God. She'd never known an attraction like this before. Of course, she'd had boyfriends. She wasn't a virgin or anything, but this was beyond anything in her experience. This was a knowing. A soul-deep yearning. It didn't seem to matter that rationally she wasn't interested in being anyone's Mate. Her body reacted to him in a way that shut down rational thought. This had nothing to do with logic.

"You'll stay here. We'll find your sister. Then you'll be on your way."

"Yep."

"Back to the States."

"Chicago."

"Good."

"Fine."

"Ah," he muttered under his breath, "bugger that."

Then he grabbed her, yanking her off the bed, swinging her into his arms and lowering his head to hers all in one smooth motion. Aly dropped her sweater and wrapped her arms around his neck to hold on as his mouth took hers in the most amazing kiss she'd ever known.

His tongue claimed hers, sweeping inside her mouth to explore, to taste, to devour. His breath dusted her cheek as she gave as well as she took. His arms, thick with muscles gained in centuries of battle, crushed her to him, until all she could feel was the outline of his body pressed along hers. His erection was full and hard and eager. She wriggled against him, giving him more, demanding more in return.

Their mouths were fused. Her hands combed through his hair, then slid down to his shoulders. The taste of him filled her, and when he groaned, it was like music. Her body went to liquid heat, and the core of her ached. He swept one hand down her spine, cupped her behind in his palm and squeezed. Now she groaned as sexual heat pumped through her veins in a rich rush of desire unlike anything she'd ever known before. She felt wild, wanted, *needed.* And there was more, so much more. The connection that had sprung up between them at a touch now seemed to wrap them together in gossamer threads that tightened as he continued his ferociously intimate assault.

That could mean only one thing. And she shuddered from the knowledge that they *were* Destined Mates.

Instantly, Rogan pulled free of her, tearing his mouth from hers, dropping her to her feet and taking a step back for good measure. "We're not."

"You were mind-reading again," she accused while trying to get her breath back and ease her heartbeat down from a frantic gallop.

"I was, yes. And your mind is a whirling mass of confusion, Alison Blair."

"Yet you managed to pull that one thought from all the rest."

He scraped one hand across his jaw and threw his hair back from his face. "It was clear enough."

"I'm right, aren't I?"

His gaze bore into hers, fire and ice. He didn't say anything, just scowled at her.

Even if you are right, it changes nothing.

"It changes everything," she argued and hardly realized she was responding to what she'd heard in his mind.

"Ah, damn it to hell and back again," he said, stalking across the room to the fireplace. He leaned both hands on the mantel, stared down into the flames and said, "You heard my thoughts."

"I…" She stopped, frowned a little and nodded, though he wasn't watching her. She had heard him. And from her work with the Society, she knew that though the Guardians were telepathic, only a Destined Mate could read a Guardian's thoughts. A sinking sensation opened up inside her as she remembered hearing Rogan order her to fall to the ground and stay there during his fight with the demon.

She'd told herself at the time that she'd imagined it. But clearly, it was more than that. There was a bond between them, and ignoring it wouldn't make it go away.

"Yeah," she admitted slowly. "I heard that thought as clear as day."

He turned his head to look at her, and in the firelight he looked downright scary. His features were hard, as if carved from stone. Only his eyes showed life, and there she found only fury shining at her. "Another link," he mused. "Another link in a chain designed to bind us together. A chain I don't want."

"Neither do I," she protested and bent to scoop up her sweater from the floor. She wished she could pull it back on, but the stupid turtleneck would probably tear the bandage off her neck and they'd have to start all over. Not a good idea.

He pushed away from the mantel, turned to face her and folded his arms across his chest. "Then we're agreed," he said quietly. "We'll not be doing that again. And there'll be no more bonding between us."

"Right." She nodded firmly and held her sweater in front of her as if it were a shield protecting her in battle. And maybe it was. "No more bonding. We find Casey. I go home."

"Good, then."

Everything in her screamed at her to go to him, to wrap her arms around him and burrow close. Fighting those instincts was exhausting, so the best thing she could do was to get herself out of temptation's way. Yes, she wanted him, but she didn't want the strings that came attached to the gorgeous warrior.

"Okay. I'm going to go to my room and change—"

He nodded and she felt his gaze on her as she quietly left the room and closed the door behind her.

* * *

Rogan's plan had failed miserably.

He'd kissed Alison in order to prove to himself that she was *not* a Destined Mate. Instead, he'd found himself caught up in the same kind of bonding he'd once known with another woman. And how was that possible, he wanted to know.

All Guardians knew that there was one Destined Mate for each of them.

One.

He'd found and lost his centuries ago. So why were his senses being battered by this American woman? How was it possible he was experiencing the bonding? How was she able to read his thoughts as easily as he read hers? He felt her presence here in his house, and it took everything in him not to go to her.

But the warrior in him refused to give sway to temptation.

Instead, he turned, as he always had, to what he did best. He headed downstairs, plucked his coat off the chair and slipped into it. As he opened the front door, though, he stopped briefly and looked up the stairs to the second floor, as if he could see through the walls to Alison, in her room.

Tension coiled within him as he stepped outside, welcoming the slap of the wind as he would have a jump into a cold lake. His blood still burned, but there was ice nipping at him now, buffering the sensations inside until they were at least tolerable.

Striding to the end of the drive, he stopped to have a word with Sean, his housekeeper's son and the gatekeeper. "Keep an eye out tonight. Stay within the gates, let no one in."

"Trouble?" Sean's brow furrowed, and his dark brown eyes peered past Rogan, looking down the drive to the road as if he could spot a legion of demons marching on the house.

Maggie's family had long served the Guardians. They'd been with him for years and were as aware of the other worlds as they were of their own. To Rogan, they were family, the only family he'd known in centuries.

"Always," Rogan said, forcing a smile before he added, "There's something more, though. Something different happening. No one goes beyond the gate at night, *no one*," he emphasized the last two words, since he wouldn't put it past Alison to try to follow him.

"No worries, Rogan. Do what you must. We'll be here."

Sean opened the gates for him, then closed and locked them once more. Iron gates wouldn't prevent a demon from slipping onto the property, but the protection spell set around the place would hold against an incursion of evil.

Satisfied, Rogan gave one last look at the house;

then muttering a curse, he walked away from the warmth and light into the cold shadows he knew so well.

He found the dead man half-hidden in the Tour-makeady Woods.

Rogan went down on one knee in the dirt, his keen eyesight sharp even in darkness. He recognized a demon kill and his senses tightened. The dead man's chest had been shredded by claws, the blood on the earth around him marred by prints that looked more animal than human. And he knew that when the authorities discovered the body, that's what they would see. They'd dismiss the kill as an animal attack. Perhaps wild dogs or some other such nonsense. But then, Rogan knew that mortals reached for normalcy when confronted with the unexplainable. They didn't want to know that there were other, far-more-dangerous creatures stalking them in the darkness.

He stood up, hand at the hilt of his sword, and scanned the area with one quick sweep of his gaze. Trace energy patterns were already dissipating in the icy wind blowing in off the Lough. But Rogan's trained eye picked out the faintest smudge of pale green drifting through the twisted woods.

He followed that trail, losing himself in the darkness. Over the years he'd learned that demons were as wide and varied as humankind. Some came onto this dimension wanting only to blend into the world, become a part of it. Others, though, desired only blood. They came here looking for victims, relishing in the hunt, as though they were sportsmen on holiday, looking for trophy kills.

This demon was one of the latter.

Rogan felt it in his bones and spared one thought for Alison's sister. He hoped to hell she hadn't come upon a demon such as this one. But if she were still alive, the question was *why?* He'd never known demons to kidnap humans. There would be no point to it.

Rogan?

He was brought up short as Alison's voice whispered into his mind. Already that bond between them was stronger. That bloody kiss had done this, he told himself and cursed fluidly in the Gaelic he was so at home with.

He'd thought to prove to himself that there was no connection. That all he and Alison shared was lust, pure and simple. But he'd only managed to make things more untenable.

Rogan, I know you can hear me, her voice came again, sliding through his mind like silk across skin. *Have you found out something about Casey?*

No. He sent that one word back to her in a silent bellow, not sure if she would hear him or not. Would the telepathic link between them be strong enough for her to read him at a distance? Or was she simply projecting her thoughts to him in the hopes of reaching him?

You were thinking about Casey just a minute ago.

So she could hear his thoughts. Bloody marvelous that was, he told himself, already erecting mental blocks so that she couldn't receive anything he didn't deliberately send to her.

Shutting me out is not an answer.

I'm on a hunt, and your mental prodding isn't a bit of a help, he pointed out, grumbling to himself even as he slipped farther into the woods after his prey.

I heard you wondering why a demon would keep Casey alive.

He didn't have to be psychically linked to her to feel her pain. Her fear. It dripped in her voice like thick honey. And a part of him wanted to comfort her.

Even as he moved through the darkness, his gaze alert, every sense aware, he sought to soothe the woman he'd left behind. Yet he couldn't lie to her, either. There was no point in her holding out hope when none might actually exist. *I've never known demons to kidnap humans. There's no point. Humans can't live in a demon dimension for more than a few days.*

I know. Pain shimmered through their link and swamped him as though her body were being immersed in an agony too deep to not share. *Casey and me, we've always been able to communicate with each other psychically, and I haven't felt her since she disappeared. But she's not dead. I'd know it if she were.*

I believe you, he assured her.

To his right, a wash of pale orange waved across the darkness, and Rogan spun, darting quickly to follow. He heard the demon's breath, harsh and strained as it ran, crashing through the trees, feet pounding against the earth as it rushed blindly in an attempt to escape him.

But there would be no escape. He'd guarded this corner of Ireland for centuries. Kept it safe. And he wouldn't fail now. Whether this demon knew of Casey or not, it would be captured and returned to its hell.

Rogan?

Be silent! The order came fast and hard. He'd no time to ease her fears at the moment. They'd talk more when he returned to the house. But for now he put the woman out of his mind and focused solely on the hunt.

Chapter 6

Watery sunlight crept into the massive kitchen the next afternoon and made Aly grateful for the brightly lit room *and* the company. The kitchen was a pale yellow with white cabinets, giving the impression of sunny cheer even on the grayest of days. And the woman who ran Rogan's household was as bright as the room itself.

About fifty, Maggie Riordan wore baggy blue jeans, a green Irish knit sweater and a white apron tied around her thick waist. Her graying red hair was cut short and flipped in the back, and her sharp blue eyes didn't miss much.

"Will you have more tea, then?" Maggie smiled and lifted the flower-bedecked teapot.

"No, thanks, Maggie. I'm sloshing already."

"Nothing like a good cuppa to set you right on a chill day."

"It is that," Aly said, shifting her gaze to the wide bay windows overlooking a sweep of grass that tumbled down a hill and ended in a stand of woods behind Rogan's house. Still farther stood the Partry Mountains, a dark purple smudge against a gray sky. The view out the front door was of the Lough, but here there was green you could find only in Ireland. So many different shades of green—it nearly made her eyes hurt to look at them all. At least that's the reason Aly gave herself for the sudden sting of tears she felt gathering in her eyes.

"The wild daffodils will be up in another week or two. It's lovely then."

Sighing, Aly turned back to look at the woman working steadily at the island counter. All day Maggie had been a whirlwind of activity. She'd dusted, vacuumed and cleaned rooms that looked as though they'd never seen a spot of dust, and for the past two hours she'd been baking. The scent of cinnamon sugar wafted in the oven-heated air and had Aly reaching for another cookie. She took a bite and said, "My sister and I won't be here for two weeks, we'll—"

She'd almost said that she and Casey would be home in Chicago in two weeks. But the words died unuttered, and the cookie tasted like sawdust in her mouth. She forced it down, convulsively swallowing because spitting it out wasn't an option.

"Ah, there now, love," Maggie said, reading Aly's expression. "You're not to worry. Rogan will be finding your sister, and all will be well. You'll see."

Lifting her teacup, Aly took a sip of the still-warm black tea and then braced the cup between her palms, feeling as though the warmth she'd felt only moments ago had drained right out of her. "I hope you're right."

"Oh," Maggie told her as she kneaded dough for fresh brown bread, "you'll find I'm always right. It's a gift. Or a curse, as himself calls it."

Aly smiled, as she'd been expected to. "You've worked for him a long time?"

"Oh, I've been with Rogan nearly thirty years," Maggie said. "He's a fine man, and I know he'll find your sister, poor darlin'. No doubt he's looking for her even now."

"He was supposed to take me with him," Aly said tightly, feeling so damn helpless she wanted to scream. Here she sat, tucked away in Rogan's house while the big, strong Guardian wandered the countryside looking for her sister. *She* should be a part of the search.

Aly fidgeted on the stool pulled up to the wide kitchen island. Bracing her elbows on the granite counter, she watched as the elder woman's strong hands twisted and pounded the thick dough. But even as she watched, her mind was busy.

Last night, after their kiss, Aly had been almost horrified by the fact that she'd been able to read Rogan's thoughts. There were too many implications to consider to make her happy about it. But then, she'd realized that reading his thoughts would allow her to know what he was doing. Where he was searching. What he was finding. But in the middle of a mental "conversation," Rogan had cut her off from his mind, shutting her out completely. And it worried her that she might not be able to read the Guardian when she needed to. What if he found something about Casey and decided not to tell her? What if he tried to keep her locked up here in his gorgeous castle of a home instead of letting her help?

She'd have no way of knowing what was going on if he continued to build mental walls against her.

"Take you with him?" Maggie repeated and gave her a wide-eyed look. "To deal with the demons, you mean? Oh, now I can't see Rogan allowing for that."

Allow. "He said he would. We made a deal."

Maggie frowned, then shrugged. "Well, then, a man of his word is Rogan. I'm sure you can believe him."

"Hmm. I'm not so sure." Aly glanced out the window again and saw the first blush of color staining the sky as sunset crept closer. "He's been gone all day without a word. Does he expect me to just sit here?"

"You were doing the research on the Internet, though, weren't you?"

"Yes," she admitted and slid off the kitchen stool to pace the room. Her sneakers squeaked against the tile as she moved. "But I haven't found anything. I should probably go to Dublin, to Society headquarters there. Maybe there's a record of this kind of thing happening before."

"The kidnappings, you mean." Maggie slapped the bread dough down onto a baking sheet, prodded it into the shape of a flat ball and then grabbed a knife. Flouring the blade, she made two quick strokes, slicing a cross in the middle of the bread. "In all my years of working for the Guardians, I've never heard the like."

"Neither had Rogan."

Maggie slid the bread into the oven to bake, and Alison started cleaning up the work surface. It felt strange to be with someone *not* a Society member and still be able to talk about demons. She was so used to lying about what she did for a living that it was actually a relief to be able to be honest.

"Everything I've checked online is coming up empty, too," Aly added with a deep sigh. "And that's what's worrying me. If something has changed in the demon world, shouldn't we know about it? The Society seer said only that something more wicked than usual was rising in Ireland."

Maggie crossed herself, then cleaned off the counter with a few quick swipes of a dishcloth. "As if the everyday demon threat wasn't enough," she muttered. "Seems to me that a man who calls himself a seer should be able to offer more information than that pitifully small nugget."

Aly leaned against the counter and nibbled at her thumbnail. When she realized what she was doing though, she stopped and stuffed her hands into her jeans pockets just for good measure. She hadn't bitten her nails in years, and she wouldn't start again now. "That's Rogan's position. He doesn't seem to have much respect for the Society at all, and far less for the seers."

Maggie glanced at her and clucked her tongue. "Rogan's a man who likes to do things himself."

"That's plenty clear," Aly mumbled. She hadn't even seen Rogan since the night before. When she woke up this morning, he'd already been gone. And he'd *stayed* gone all day. It was as if the legendary Guardian was actually hiding from her.

Now it was nearly twilight again. Obviously, he was avoiding her, doing a good job of it, too. But just how long did he plan to keep it up? What had happened to their bargain? The one sealed with a kiss hot enough that even the memory of his mouth on hers was enough to curl her toes?

"I know you're worried for your sister," Maggie said, her voice softly sympathetic. "And who wouldn't be? But as there's nothing you can do, don't make yourself sick over this. Why don't..."

Aly?

Casey's oh-so-familiar voice whispered into her mind. Aly came up and away from the counter as if she'd been shot. Staring blindly around the kitchen, she heard Maggie talking, though her voice was no more than a buzz of words barely understood.

Instead, Alison focused her energies inside, willing her sister to call to her again. *Casey? Casey, where are you?*

Silence streamed into her mind, and the emptiness chilled Aly to the bone. Had she only imagined the sound of her sister's mind touching hers? Was she so desperate for word on Casey that her own imagination was providing respite? She rubbed her forehead and only half heard as Maggie moved about the kitchen, still speaking.

Help me, Aly. Oh, God. Help me.

Adrenaline pumped through Aly's body as though shot from a fire hose. It was real. Casey was out there. Alive. And she needed help. *I'm coming, honey. Hang on, I'm coming.*

Then she came out of her thoughts, looked at

Maggie, who was staring at her in concern, and said, "I'm sorry. What did you say?"

Instantly, Maggie came to her, gave Aly's shoulders a quick squeeze and said, "Why don't you go on up and lie down for a bit. You're worn to the bone with worry. A rest will likely do you a world of good."

Kind, kind woman, Aly thought and briefly experienced a flash of guilt. But it was gone a heartbeat later. Casey was what mattered here. Casey needed her, and Aly could do nothing but go to her. "Good idea." She headed for the door, then stopped as if an idea had just popped into her head. "You know, I think I'll go outside. Take a walk before the sun goes down."

Immediately, Maggie threw a glance at the windows and, seeing that sunset was barely begun, she nodded. "Why don't you do that. I often stand down by the Lough. Clears a body's mind to stare out at the water and feel the wind slicing at you."

Aly nodded, grateful for the kindness and for the fact that Maggie was clearly far too nice a woman to suspect that Aly might be lying to her. "I'll be back soon."

She stopped at a closet in the hall, pulled her jacket down and quickly threw it on. If she was going to get past Maggie's son, Sean, at the gate, she had to hurry. *Casey, where are you?*

A moment passed, then two. Finally though,

Casey's thoughts came through in a soft, tired stream that seemed to be fading even as Aly listened.

By the lake, I think. In a castle. Ruins.

Aly was out the front door and headed down the drive at a sprint, holding on to Casey's spirit with an iron fist. Whatever she'd gone through, whatever she'd experienced or seen, it didn't matter. All that mattered was that she was alive. And Aly was going to make sure her little sister stayed that way.

Overhead, gray clouds raced across the sky, allowing small flashes of blue to peek through briefly before covering them up again. The wind pushed at her, as if an unseen hand was trying to force her back into the house. But Aly hurried on, only stopping when Sean stepped in front of the closed gates, arms folded over his chest.

"Where you off to, miss?"

"Just a walk, Sean," Aly said, disguising the sense of urgency clawing at her. She had to get past Rogan's guard dog if she were to help Casey. "Down to the lake and back."

He shook his head, frowning, and a quick bubble of panic rose up inside her. "Rogan wants no one going out."

"At night," Aly corrected. "Your mom told me that Rogan wants us staying inside the house at night. But it's not dark yet. Sunset's barely getting started."

He shot a look at the sky as if to confirm what she'd said, and what he saw made the frown on his face ease up just a bit. His hesitation gave Aly the break she was hoping for. She smiled at him, forcing herself to speak slowly, as if there were no hurry. As if her sister's life didn't depend on her escaping the house.

"Look," she said with what she hoped looked like a casual shrug, "I'm going stir-crazy inside. I **just need a** little walk. I'll be back before dark. I swear."

Aly, I need you...

Alison's insides jumped at the soft, frail sound of her sister's voice echoing through her mind. It was so not like Casey to sound so...defeated. Beaten.

"All right, then," he said, though he shook his head as if he were mentally arguing with himself. "But you get yourself back before sunset."

"Oh, I will," she promised, not caring that it might very well be a lie. Of course she'd try to get back quickly. No way did she want to run into a demon. But if she had to stay out the whole damn night to somehow protect Casey, then that's what she'd do. As soon as Sean unlocked the gates, Aly sprinted through them, following the drive down the sloping path to the Lough.

Casey, hang on, honey.

Silence answered her and Aly ran harder. Faster.

For all she knew, Casey lay dying. Alone. Afraid. Oh, God. Casey couldn't die. She was all the family Aly had left. While Aly ran and her brain taunted her with the thought of everything that could go wrong, she reached instinctively for Rogan's mind. He'd shut her out, keeping her from reading him somehow, but she knew the warrior could still hear *her.*

He was the one person she knew who could help. And for the first time since she'd felt those tiny threads of connection spinning out between them, she was grateful for it.

Rogan.

Just thinking his name helped. Remembering that he was there to be called on.

I need you, she whispered, trembling at the words that rocked her to her soul. She *did* need him, desperately, at the moment. She needed not only his strength and prowess but also his comfort. She needed to hear the sound of his voice in her mind, to calm the ragged edge of the control she felt slipping from her fingers. Her sister was hurt. Scared. Counting on her.

Rogan, answer me!

Panic underlined her thoughts as she reached into the emptiness, straining to find him.

At the edge of the Lough, Aly looked wildly around in the waning light. The water in Lough Mask churned with the wind and slapped against the shore. Fishing boats that were anchored near a short dock rocked and creaked, sounding like nails on a chalkboard. Rocks and dirt shifted beneath Aly's feet as she stopped long enough to catch her breath. To her left, up a green slope, sat the B and B she and Casey had stayed in so briefly. New spring lambs jumped and frolicked in the fenced front pasture, and in the distance a dog barked.

Ahead of her lay a hill, and at its peak were the ruins of an ancient keep. She'd seen them her first day in Ireland and had, for some reason, averted her gaze almost instantly. There was something about the place…a darkness that pulled and tugged at her. Now, staring up at the tumbled stones that marked the grave of a castle that had once stood tall and proud, Aly felt her soul cringe. Everything in her screamed at her to stay away, to keep her distance. But she couldn't.

Casey was there.

She felt it.

Bracing her hands on her knees, she sucked in air and mentally reached for Rogan again. He wasn't answering her, but she knew he heard her. Knew that he was still keeping her locked out of reading his thoughts. For the first time, she was grateful for the connection between them. She had no interest in being a Destined Mate to a Guardian, but she wasn't stupid, either. She'd use whatever she could to help her save her sister. Even if that meant tying herself however briefly to an arrogant warrior who wouldn't deign to answer her calls.

Rogan! Rogan, you can hear me. You must answer! I've left the house. I'm going to Casey.

Instantly, his thunderous roar filled her mind. *You cannot.*

Too late.

She ran, not willing to stand still and have a mental argument, since the sun was sinking, spreading brilliant colors of red and violet across the sky. The clouds lit up as if they were on fire, and darkness crouched, at the ready.

Return to the house. I am coming.

No. Her legs ached, and she made a mental note to exercise more once this was over. She ran, stumbling in the damp grass, and spoke to Rogan. *Casey's alive. I heard her. She needs help and I'm going to her.*

Do not! His order came into her mind instantly and she felt his power surrounding her.

Just the sound of his voice in her mind steeled her for whatever she might have to face in the coming minutes.

You can't stop me. Besides, I'm almost there. Not that she would have turned around even if she weren't.

Where? Tell me where.

The ruins above the Lough. She said she was in the ruins. Aly stopped halfway up the hill, her lungs laboring, her knees trembling. But she hadn't stopped just to catch her breath. She was fighting for every step now. The closer she came to the ruins, the more her body fought her. As if her very bones were trying to force her to back away.

To run.

She shivered, turned for a look back down the way she'd come and saw that the sky was deepening. Night was almost on her, and she didn't have Casey safe yet. This was why she'd come alone, not able to wait for Rogan to join her. If she hadn't come when she had, Casey would be alone in the dark. Terrified. Traumatized. She couldn't allow that to happen.

Her gaze swept back to the blackened stones in front of her, and she thought she felt a desperate sigh on the wind. The sound of weeping.

I'll join you there. Irritation came across with his thoughts, and Aly knew she would later have to face a furious Guardian. *Do nothing else. Find your sister and stay at the ruins. Wait for me.*

No problem, she assured him. She wasn't a complete idiot. Aly knew that she was no match for whatever creatures preyed on the countryside in the darkness. And the very thought of entering those ruins filled her with a cold dread that had her teeth chattering. Yet she had to go, had to face whatever was there. For Casey.

Clinging to the fact that Rogan was on his way,

Aly continued the climb up the slope and concentrated on the skeletal remains of the once-proud castle looming ahead of her. In the dusky light those stones seemed alive. Every inch of Ireland was crowded with ghosts, with the echoes of lives lived and lost over the centuries.

And here, Aly thought as she struggled for breath, the ghosts were thick.

She stumbled across the ground and fell, landing on a rock that sliced through her jeans and gashed her knee. But pain was no more than background noise in the rush of sensations pouring over her.

Déjà vu.

Where it came from, Aly had no idea. She'd never been here before. Had, in fact, avoided looking at the place since her arrival in Ireland. But she *knew* this place.

Faded images rushed through her mind in a whirlwind of color and sound. She felt as if she were drowning in the outpouring of emotions swamping her. In one beat of her heart, she felt joy and pain and fear and regret and so many other frenzied bursts of emotion that she couldn't separate one from the next.

Her breath strangled in her lungs. Her eyes filled and tears streamed unchecked down her face as she turned helplessly in a circle. Her gaze swept the charred ruins. The tumbled stones themselves seemed to cry out in agony for what had been lost.

And Aly was powerless to stop any of it. She clapped both hands to her head and groaned as images rose and fell in her mind. Snow-filled days. The clash of swords. Stone hearths dancing with flames. Green eyes staring into hers. Screams. Shouts. And the soul-tearing sound of broken sobs echoing through the centuries.

Her psychic abilities had never been this strong. She'd never been one to pick up on images, or ghostly fields. As a member of the Society, she was psychic, but generally that ability only stretched to allow her to sense a Guardian's presence and to read the trace energy patterns of demons. She'd only ever felt a connection with her sister—and now, Rogan. But this was different. This wasn't *hearing*.

This was *being*.

And it was killing her.

"Stop," she whispered brokenly as she staggered across the rocky ground. Shaking her head, she willed the images into submission and even as they all washed away, like an incoming tide sweeping back out to a churning sea, she felt their power still quivering within her. There, hidden at the bottom of her soul, waiting for the chance to rise up and bring her down again.

"Oh, God, *stop*," she pleaded, knowing there was no one to hear.

She lifted her head, ignored the pounding of

what felt like dozens of tiny hammers behind her eyes and swept the interior of the ruins. Meadow grass had reclaimed the knoll. It sprang up between the weatherworn stones and obscured most of the ground. Shadows filled the corners as darkness began to inexorably swallow the site.

Overhead, the sun was in its last fiery gasp. Colors softened, the first stars poked through the layers of clouds and the wind…the wind sighed and whistled through the ruins, sounding like weeping.

"Casey!" Aly shouted, her voice startling two birds into flight, their wings a blur of motion in the dim light. "Casey, where are you?"

"Here…"

Aly heard her sister's call, so soft she'd nearly missed it beneath the moan of the wind. She ran toward the sound. Climbing over stones, stumbling on the rocks, Aly clambered over a corner of the ruined keep and finally found her sister, lying curled up on herself, back to the rocks, staring at nothing.

"Oh, God. Casey. Casey, are you all right?" Aly dropped to her knees and fought the impulse to grab her sister and hold her close. If she was injured, though, Aly could do her more damage. So while she whispered soothing words in a sing-songy tone, she ran her hands up and down her sister's body.

The red T-shirt and black skirt Casey had worn to the pub, seemingly a lifetime ago, now were dirty, torn. And not nearly enough to keep her warm. Her arms were covered in small cuts and bruises. Her eyes were wide and glassy, her skin too pale, with a bluish tinge.

Panic reared its ugly head as Aly shrugged out of her coat and laid it over Casey. Instantly, she felt the icy fingers of the wind. She turned her face into it, letting that cold force push her hair out of her eyes. Darkness was almost complete now, and the spooky sensations she'd experienced just walking onto the site of the ruins intensified.

Probably her imagination again, but she felt as if there were *things* out there, watching. A prickling on her skin made her rub her arms briskly even as she silently called to Rogan.

I found her. She looks bad, Rogan. I need you here.

Do not turn your back on her, he ordered, and Aly heard the carefully banked fury in his voice. *Protect yourself, Alison. We've no idea where she's been or what's been done to her.*

She's hurt, Rogan. I think she's in shock, too. She's not going to be hurting me. She's my sister, for God's sake.

Gaelic curses filled her mind, rich and ripe and rolling over and over each other until they sounded like a single word, spoken with a venomous temper.

Then she heard, *If it's a demon she's been with, there's no telling what's going to happen. Keep watch. Keep safe. I'm almost there.*

She felt his withdrawal and wished he'd stayed a firm presence in her mind. Aly wanted the security of knowing that he was listening, that he could touch her at will. The darkness edged closer to the ruined keep, and Aly blew out a breath as she turned her head to look down at Casey.

The blue cast to her skin was still present, despite the fact that Casey was now warmer beneath Aly's jacket. But even as she realized it, Aly knew that the faint wash of blue on her sister's flesh wasn't from the cold at all.

It was the palest remnants of a demon energy trace.

Aly's mouth went dry. Her breath came a little faster as she wondered if the demon energy clung to Casey because she'd been trapped in a demon dimension.

Or if there was another, far more terrifying reason.

"Casey?" Her voice whispered into the wind, hardly more than a sigh of sound.

As if in answer to that call, Casey opened her eyes and gave Alison a terrible smile. "I knew you'd come. I told him you would."

Fear spun through her, uncoiling in the pit of her stomach and sending ribbonlike tendrils of cold throughout Aly's body. She couldn't tear her gaze from Casey's eyes. The pupils were huge, so large and deep and black they almost obliterated the pale blue irises.

Inching backward, Aly stretched out her hands behind her, feeling the ground, clearing her path, while Casey slowly sat up, letting Aly's jacket drop to the dirt beside her. "Casey? What is it? What's happening?"

"You're about to die, Aly," Casey said, that awful smile curving her mouth.

"What?" Shock, pure and simple, had her stopping her backward motion. She stared into her younger sister's strange eyes and saw her own death written in the blackness.

"My master wants your death. And I'm bound to serve." Casey cooed the words, as if murmuring a lullaby.

"Casey, no. You don't want to do this."

"I do, Aly," her sister argued, pushing to her feet and throwing her arms wide. "I want him to be proud of me. To love me."

"Who? Who wants this? Who do you want to love you, Casey?" Aly moved again, struggling to get to her feet while keeping a wary eye on the sister she hardly recognized. Cold wind sliced to the bone, but Casey seemed unaware.

"Balam." His name came like a prayer from Casey's lips.

A demon. Of course it was a demon. Casey was covered in the trace energy colors, pale blue shining on her as if it were an aura. Aly shuddered and clambered over a couple of the stones, always watching. Always mindful. The woman across from her wasn't the sister she knew. This was a stranger. A dangerous stranger. *Rogan! Hurry, Rogan! She's not herself!*

Fight. That single word resounded over and over again in her mind, and Aly knew he was right. Staring at her sister, in the dim light of a nearly moonless sky, she saw madness. Obsession. And resolve.

Whoever Balam was, he wanted Aly dead.

And Casey was determined to make that happen.

"Why, honey?" Aly asked the question and kept her mind open to Rogan, hoping that even if he weren't contacting her, he was still listening, keyed into her thoughts. "Why does this Balam want me dead?"

Casey grinned and ran her tongue across her bottom lip. "You're to be a message. To the Guardian."

Aly swallowed hard and shifted quick glances to either side of her, ensuring she had a clear path all around her. "What kind of message?"

"Balam has plans," Casey said, wagging her index finger in a no-no-no gesture. "And he won't be stopped. Your death tells the Guardian to back off or more will die."

"That won't work," Aly said, trying to think. Trying to stay calm even while planning how to fight her sister. "Rogan won't be stopped. Killing me gains you nothing. Gains this Balam nothing."

"He is all," Casey whispered, eyes glittering, "and you *will* die."

When Casey charged her, Aly was ready. Every self-defense course she'd ever taken at the Society came crashing back to her. She remembered moves; she remembered avoidance techniques and the high kicks that used to make her insane.

She'd hated practicing. Hated the ritual, the repetition, the constant rehearsing of moves and countermoves.

And now she was immensely grateful for all of it.

Casey had never had any training, but the feral light in her eyes and the madness shining within gave her power and strength. She attacked, swiping sharpened nails toward Aly's face, and Aly quickly dropped, swung out her right leg and swept Casey's feet out from under her.

But Casey was up again in a moment. She ran at Aly, bent low, arms wide as if trying to tackle her. But Aly moved like a matador, giving Casey a push to send her crashing past her. She landed in a painful heap against the stones, and everything in Aly wanted to comfort, to help. She was forced to fight her own instincts as well as the sister she hardly recognized.

Casey screamed her frustration, and the high-pitched shriek bounced off the stones and echoed in the otherwise stillness. A chill scraped along Aly's spine as she moved in a slow circle, counter-clockwise to Casey. As she walked, she spoke, quietly, urgently. "Casey, honey, don't do this. Can't you see this isn't you? You don't want to hurt me. You love me, Casey. I love you, honey. We can fix this."

Casey didn't answer—she didn't have to. Aly read what she was thinking on her expression. Her mouth was tight and grim. Her eyes continued to fill with black until even the whites of her eyes had been obliterated now. Whatever had claimed Casey was taking her over in inches.

Death hung over the ruins like a fog. Ancient death clung to these stones, and now there was the promise of more. Casey wouldn't be dissuaded. Wouldn't be talked down or made to change what was left of her mind.

Aly had come here to save her sister. Now, to save herself, she might be forced to kill her only family.

Chapter 7

Fear.

For the first time in hundreds of years, Rogan knew the taste of fear.

Its bitter tang filled his mouth as he ran across the meadow, black hair streaming out behind him. He carried his sword, and the glint of the gleaming metal caught his eye as he ran. He had to be in time to use that sword. Had to reach Alison before— Why the bloody hell had she left his house? If she'd listened to him, this wouldn't be happening.

And if he hadn't closed his mind to hers, he would have known when she left his house, would have been able to stop her before she came into danger. Fury churned in his gut and spilled out to slide through his veins.

Along with his own terror, he felt Alison's terror, her grief, her reluctance to hurt her younger sister. Locked to her mind, he was one with her, and that was the only thing keeping him sane as he raced through the darkness.

Alison was alive.

And she would remain so.

In life his speed had been legendary among his people, his long legs and incredible endurance allowing him to run faster and longer than any others in his clan. As an Immortal his strength and his speed were further enhanced. He could, when necessary, move faster than the human eye could track. Now, he needed that speed and that endurance.

He'd just arrived back at his house when Alison's desperate call sounded in his mind. Leaving the car, he'd run across the fields and woods, using his powerful strength to make himself no more than a blur of movement through the encroaching night. Every step pounded on the turf and rattled through his body. Every step brought him closer to Alison and to the frantic battle she fought.

At the crown of the hill, he leaped across the fallen stones of the ruined keep and joined the fight just as Casey hurled a rock at Alison's head. Inserting himself between the women, Rogan knocked the stone aside with one sweep of his arm and sent it clattering to the ground.

Casey screamed and her eyes wheeled black. Her expression shifted and changed, her breath shook her body and the blue demon energy clinging to her trembled with the force of her anger.

The young woman covered in cuts and bruises flew at him, arms extended, fingers curled into claws.

"Don't hurt her!" Alison's shout filled the old keep, and the pain in her voice sliced at Rogan as surely as a blade would have.

He easily deflected Casey's ineffective attack, giving her a push that sent her sprawling to the ground. She was no warrior. She possessed no demon strength. All she had driving her was the madness seeded deeply in her mind.

He read her thoughts and found only a whirling black mass filled with the order to kill Alison. And even as he read her, he sensed something else, something human, struggling to reassert itself. Casey was strong, as strong as her sister. And she was fighting the black compulsion driving her.

Keeping his gaze locked on Casey, he shouted to Alison. "Stay back. Stand where you are."

"Rogan—"

"I'll not hurt her," he said, more quietly this time. "You've my word on it. But stand back. Your presence only feeds the madness."

Casey stared up at him, wiped a trail of blood off her chin with the back of her hand and sneered. "You think to stop my master? You're nothing."

"And you're a foolish child," he muttered, knowing he wouldn't be using his sword this night. There would be no more death on this ancient ground. Dipping one hand into his coat pocket, he kept an eye on Casey as she tried to sidle past him, her gaze locked hungrily on Alison.

Pulling the Guardian net free of his coat, he tossed it high into the air. The finely linked silver chains shone brightly in the night for a moment, then settled to earth and trapped Casey even as she futilely tried to escape.

Caught, Casey could do no more than howl and shriek ineffective curses. She twisted and writhed on the ground, and every movement she made only tightened the strength of the net surrounding her. Rogan walked closer, then went down on one knee beside the woman. She spat at him as she fought to claw herself free.

"Who do you serve?" he asked and dipped into her seething mind while he waited for her to speak.

"Balam. He who will defeat you." Her voice scratched and scraped on the air, a harsh sound of pain and fear and fury.

Rogan laughed loudly and long, and though there was no real humor in the sound, it was enough to prod the young woman into new fits of desperation. She twisted in the net's implacable grip and shouted threats and promises as to what she would do once freed.

And despite the invective, Rogan sensed Casey's true nature, still struggling to reassert itself. He would find a way to help her.

"You waste your breath and my time," he said, standing up again. Dismissing the woman for the moment, he turned instead to look at Alison.

Her features were as white as paper, her eyes wide in shock and pain. He watched as she stumbled closer to her sister, moving as if her legs were too numb to hold her. Reaching out one hand to Casey, she would have tried to touch her, but Rogan caught her small hand in his and stopped her.

"You'll not go near her," he said.

Instantly, Alison's eyes flashed at him. "She's my sister. I have to help her."

"Your sister's mind is lost in a sea of black." Frowning, he watched as his words struck her like a physical blow. "She can't hear you. Can't see you. All she sees is the victim she was sent to find."

Alison shook her head, trying to deny what he was saying. What she'd already seen for herself. "Casey wouldn't hurt me."

"*Your sister* wouldn't harm you, no. But what she is now will happily destroy you, given half a chance. I won't allow that."

Pulling her hand free of his, Alison pushed her

hair back from her face and wiped away the tears coursing freely down her cheeks. Her gaze shifted from him to her sister and back again.

Her lower lip trembled, and tears fell like raindrops on a windowpane, sliding down her cheeks in silent misery. Everything in him turned over. His anger drained away and though he hated that he cared, he couldn't deny it. At least not to himself.

He reached out and pulled her to him, enfolding her in his arms. Holding her tightly, he rested his chin on top of her head and felt her fear trembling through her.

"God, Rogan," she whispered, her voice almost lost to him, "she meant to kill me."

"Aye, she did. But she failed."

Tipping her head back, Alison stared up at him, and Rogan was briefly lost in the glimmer of tears blurring her blue eyes. A woman's best weapon, he thought, knowing he would rather face an army of screaming demons than one strong woman's tears.

"What can we do?" she asked, looking up at him, expecting him to have the answers she needed so badly. "How do we help her?"

He looked back at Casey, still struggling futilely to escape the net. His gaze moved over the fallen stones, the ruin of the walls that had long ago stood tall and straight and impenetrable.

Rogan hadn't set foot on this ground in more than four hundred years. And though he'd made his home close by, he'd taught himself to ignore this site's existence. The past clung to these stones like moss on rocky ground, and the whispers of remembrances choked him.

Standing here, he felt the past grab at him, trying to pull him down into memories that felt as fresh as yesterday.

But Alison was here, too, anchoring him in the present. He felt the warmth of her as she leaned into his strength. Felt her fear, her hesitation and could do nothing but try to ease the pain welling inside her. She needed him, needed him to somehow make this right.

As a Guardian it was his duty to protect her. Although, had it been his duty to walk away, he knew he would not have. He could no more leave her now than he could sprout wings and fly.

She was waiting, staring at him with both hope and fear shining in her eyes. He answered that plea with a vow.

"We defeat the demon."

The room was empty.

Alison felt the cold night pressing against the narrow windowpanes set into the gray stone walls and wished the light in the room were brighter. She wanted brilliant light to chase away the shadows, to keep the darkness at bay.

But there wasn't enough light in the world to shatter the darkness inside her.

There was no furniture in this small, turret room at the corner of Rogan's home. No chairs, no tables, no carpet to soften the hardwood floor. No lamps, only a single bulb shining from a globed fixture high on the ceiling. In the pale wash of light, Alison stared down at her sister, bound hand and foot and lying on the floor.

Casey's bare heels drummed on the floor in a rhythmic staccato that sounded like a frantic heartbeat. Her dirty, dark blond hair spread out beneath her head, and her black eyes continually rolled, as if she were looking beyond her stone prison to the demon that had so corrupted her.

Unearthly sounds tore from Casey's throat as she twisted helplessly from side to side as if trying to escape not only her bonds but also herself. She was caught in a trap set by a demon—and her cell was her own body.

"Oh, Casey…"

Heart breaking, Alison flinched as Casey's face contorted, becoming a vicious mask Alison didn't even recognize. Her lips peeled back from her teeth and a long, slow hiss escaped Casey's throat. "You can't keep me. You can't stop me. My master commands and I obey…"

She couldn't take this. Couldn't stand watching her little sister tormented. Couldn't bear knowing that this was all *her* fault. If she hadn't brought Casey to Ireland with her…if she'd insisted that

Casey accompany her to Rogan's house on that first, fateful night…if she had somehow been able to connect with Casey's mind before the demon had changed her…

If, if, if.

So many ifs.

So many lost chances.

And now her sister was being ruined from the inside out. Her soul conquered, her mind shattered.

Clapping one hand to her mouth to hold back the sobs that ripped at her throat, Aly whirled around, bolted from the room and slammed the door behind her. The heavy oak panel shuddered into place, and Aly turned the long brass key jutting from the lock. Then resting her forehead against the door, she let the tears come. Let them fall as her shoulders shook and her gasping breath pushed in and out of her lungs.

Her hair hung on either side of her face, a blond curtain, giving her the illusion of solitude in the long hallway, narrowing her view to the door in front of her. Her gaze was blurred with tears she couldn't block. Her throat ached with the strain of holding back the sobs that wanted to shake free. Her entire being throbbed, as if every cell in her body were being attacked by an unseen force.

She had never felt more alone.

You are not alone.

Rogan's voice whispered into her mind, easing

the fear, soothing the pain. She lifted her head, blinked away her tears and stared down the long, dimly lit hallway to the closed door of his room at the far end of the passage.

As she watched, the door opened and Rogan stood in the doorway, backlit from the room behind him. He was impossibly tall and broad and exuded strength. Something she needed badly at the moment.

But it was more than that and Aly knew it.

She needed *him*.

Then come to me, his voice beckoned, a promise in her mind.

He lifted one hand to her and Aly started walking. Every step was quicker than the last until she was nearly running down the hall, her bare feet making almost no sound at all on the thick carpet runner covering the bare wood floors. Her vision blurred again as her tears kept pace with her steps. Her breath heaved in and out of her lungs, her stomach flip-flopped with nerves and her heart beat out a sure rhythm telling her she was doing exactly the right thing.

She hadn't wanted to become involved with a Guardian, hadn't wanted to admit that what she felt for Rogan was complex and confusing and over-whelming. But tonight, when the world around her seemed darker and far more dangerous than it ever had…when her only family in the world was being tormented by a demon too cowardly to do its own dirty work…when the gleam in Rogan's green eyes was the only safe harbor she could find, she gave herself up to it.

And to hell with what came after.

She flew into his arms. He lifted her off her feet and held her while she all but crawled up his body as though she were climbing a mountain. Burying her face in the curve of his neck, she finally let all of her tears come, knowing that he would hold her, protect her.

His big hands swept up and down her back as he moved into his bedroom, kicking the door closed behind them. The lights were low, and the crackle and hiss of the fire in the hearth sounded like hushed, comforting whispers. She locked her legs around his middle and clung to him as though he were a lifeline tossed to her as she struggled to keep from drowning.

"It's not tears she needs from you now, Alison."

"I've nothing else to give her," Aly choked out. "I can't reach her. I talk to her and she hisses at me."

"The demon's poisoned your sister's mind. He's a hold on her now and won't be letting go without a fight."

She pulled her head back just enough so that she could look into his eyes. That brilliant green stared back at her, and a wisp of a memory floated dizzily through her mind and was gone again in a heartbeat, leaving her feeling as though there was something she should know, something she should feel. But her heart ached in her chest, and she didn't care to try to figure it out.

"How do we fight the demon without hurting Casey?"

He walked, carrying her, to the edge of his bed and sat down, cradling her in his lap. Aly squirmed around until she was comfortable and didn't even smile when he groaned just a bit at all of her moving around. Then, leaning her head against his chest, she listened to the steady beat of his heart and tried to match her own to his. This was comfort. What she'd needed. What she could find only with him.

Who else in the world would understand what was happening? She couldn't go to the Garda to complain about a demon possession. They'd lock her up. No, Rogan was her only hope—Casey's only hope.

From down the hall, she heard a long, piteous howl of pain and desperation, and Alison closed her eyes, cringing from the knowledge that her little sister was tied up in an empty room.

"Listen to her," she whispered, feeling the shattered fragments of her heart splinter even further.

"No," he said softly, "don't. She's lost in her own world now, is Casey. There's no reaching her yet."

"Rogan," she whispered, her words coming thick

and raw from a throat that felt as though it were on fire. "Rogan, she looks at me and doesn't even know me."

He shook his head, a sad knowing in his eyes. "A part of her knows, even now. And a part of her fights. But the demon's got a strong hold on her, and to save her we must break it—if we can."

"I'm so scared," Aly said softly, admitting to the terror within. His arms tightened around her, and she let herself enjoy the warmth, the power in his hold. In his arms she felt secure, safe from a world that was suddenly more terrifying than anything she could have imagined.

Rogan slid one huge hand up and down her back in an effort to comfort, but it wasn't comfort she was feeling. It was the buzz of her blood, pumping thickly through her veins. This closeness with him was dissolving from reassurance into something more. Something vital.

Her breath shuddered in and out of her lungs as she looked up at him. His green eyes glittered, and she knew he was feeling exactly what she was. And suddenly, Aly needed him. Needed him as she needed her next breath.

Lifting one hand, she cupped his cheek and felt the scrub of a day's worth of whiskers bristle against her palm. He snaked in a quick breath and held himself perfectly still. Her fingers speared through his long, thick hair, and she loved the feel of it against her skin.

She squirmed around on his lap again and felt beneath her, the thick, heavy proof of his need pressing against her bottom.

He drew another sharp, quick breath. "I beg you to sit still, Alison Blair," he said through gritted teeth. "If you've a generous bone in that body, you'll be still for sweet Christ's sake."

"No," she said, pulling his head to hers. "I don't want to be still. I want to feel the fire, Rogan. I want to feel something more than…fear."

He looked down into her blue eyes and knew himself for a lost man. He hadn't meant to be close to her again. To kiss her again. And now, he knew if he didn't have her, bury himself inside her damp heat…that his immortal life wouldn't be worth living.

A rumbling growl roared up from his chest as he scooped her up, stood, then laid her out on the wide bed. Stripping out of his clothes, Rogan felt her gaze on him, the power in it. The hunger. And it fed his own.

Keeping her gaze fixed with his, Alison tugged her sweater off, then undid the snap and zipper of her jeans. He pulled them down her legs and off, tossing them to the floor. Then she wore nothing but an ivory lace bra and panties. Her skin was the color of rich cream. Her eyes shone in the lamplight and he found himself staring deep.

"Take them off," he ordered, his voice rough with need.

Still watching him, Aly did as he said. Her tongue swept along her bottom lip, and Rogan's erection jumped in eager anticipation. She smiled knowingly, then unhooked the clasp at the center of her chest. Slowly, teasingly, she slid out of her bra, freeing her breasts to his gaze.

Not small, not large, they were perfect, firm and soft, with rose-petal nipples that were hard now with her own hunger and the chill in the room.

"Now the panties," he growled, keeping a tight leash on the hunger that roared within. He wanted to see all of her, explore every inch of her.

She took a long, deep breath and planted her feet on the mattress. Lifting her hips, she hooked her thumbs in the elastic band of the pale lace panties and slowly, languidly, peeled them off. He snatched them from her hand, tossed them behind him, and when she would have shifted position, lowering her legs again, he held her in place.

While she watched him, he reached for her core. With one finger alone, he slowly stroked her damp folds. One finger slid over and into her, dipping, exploring.

She gasped and lifted her hips. "Rogan, this is no time to tease me…"

He caught her gaze and smiled as he watched her eyes glitter. "You're wrong. 'Tis the perfect time."

He found her heat and loved the feel of it. He slid another finger into her depths as he stood at the edge of the bed and looked down at her delectable naked body. His own body ached and throbbed for release, but he would have this first. He would watch her slide over. See the storm clouds gather in her eyes and feel the rush of completion as it swamped her.

Then, he would claim his own release.

Taking hold of her legs, he pulled her close to the edge of the mattress, and when he had her where he wanted her, he scooped both hands under her bottom and lifted her clean off the bed. Legs dangling, helpless in his grasp, she looked up at him as he lowered his mouth to taste her.

"Rogan!"

His mouth covered her. His tongue dipped into her slick heat and tasted the very essence of her. She arched into him, her hips twisting in his firm hold. But he gave her no release, gave her no end to the sensations coursing through her. Instead, he took her higher.

He nibbled, he stroked, he suckled. He felt every one of her responses like a shudder through his own body. His hands squeezed her bottom as he held her to his mouth and gave himself over to the wonder of the woman in his bed.

Her gasps and half-uttered cries filled the room that had been empty for too long. Her sighs drifted into him, filling up corners of his heart, his soul, that he'd believed were better off empty. And the heat of her body soaked into his, driving away the relentless cold he'd lived with for so long.

She stiffened against him, arching high and proud, jutting her breasts toward heaven as he sent her tumbling into paradise with a quick stroke of his tongue.

Before the last of the tremors shivered through her, he lowered her hips, held her in place and pushed his body into hers. She gasped as he filled her, and he groaned, a deep, rich sound of ecstasy. She took him all, sheathing him in a tight, hot fist of sensation. To the hilt, he buried himself within and paused for several seconds to simply revel in the rightness of it.

"Rogan," she said as he moved within her slowly, deliberately, stroking her inside as he rubbed that one wild spot of tenderness above her core. "I can't. Not so soon. I can't take another one like the last one…"

"You can and you will," he promised, staring into her eyes, pumping his body with hard, deep thrusts.

And despite what she claimed, she hooked her legs around his middle and pulled him tighter, deeper inside. Her hips rocked, her hands fisted in the duvet beneath her. Her head twisted from side to side, and her tongue swept out to moisten dry lips. He watched her helpless writhing, felt the swamping need in her mind and let her passions guide his own.

Sheathed within her, he knew he would never be able to be deep enough. He would always want more. Need more.

Again and again, he thrust into her depths, and she met him eagerly, move for move. They came together, their bodies linked, and as he moved in and out of her heat, he felt the silky tendrils of a bonding take place. The fragile, invisible threads wound themselves around the two of them, linking Rogan and Alison more firmly together.

He mentally railed against what was happening. It could not be true. Alison Blair couldn't possibly be his Destined Mate, despite what his body was telling him, despite the fact that their minds reached for each other. And yet, he felt his strength, his power, grow immeasurably as his body joined with hers.

Her eyes went wide as he shouted her name, body erupting, emptying inside her with the force of a man long denied. And with a flick of his thumb, he took her with him onto that steep slide into oblivion. He felt her body tremble, heard her call his name and felt her inner muscles work on him as she went through a climax as overwhelming as his own.

Aly's body felt as though it had shattered into a million pieces. But her mind was even more splintered. She struggled for breath as she tried to make sense of the images, thoughts and memories crowding her brain. *Memories.* Of a different time. A different place.

She looked up at Rogan looming over her, his body still locked deep within hers, and as she watched him, the world shifted, changed, became something else. Something…that couldn't be.

They were in a meadow, naked in the cold night, lying on a blanket spread atop the grass. Behind them the castle stood tall and proud, torchlight burning in the window apertures and arrow slits. Sounds crashed over her. The wind on the lake, night birds calling to each other. A woman in the distance, singing, and an infant's hungry wail.

Rogan's long black hair streamed out behind him in the wind as he smiled at her, a roguish curve of his mouth. She reached for him with hands that weren't hers. A thick ring with a cabochon ruby winked at her in the moonlight as she stroked Rogan's sculpted chest.

He tweaked one of her nipples and she laughed, the sound deep and throaty. She looked into his eyes and saw her own reflection staring back at her—but it was a woman she didn't know.

An instant later, those memories shifted again, rippling like the surface of a pond after a stone had been tossed into it. *She saw Rogan, wearing a leather battle vest, his long hair clubbed at the back*

*of his neck, astride a war horse. And she saw
herself, running from him in sheer terror.*

"Oh, God." She swallowed hard as her mind
tried to explain away what she was feeling. Her
heart pounded in her chest as she fought to squirm
out from under Rogan. She needed to be apart from
him. "Get off. Get off me, Rogan. Please."

He did. Pulling free of her, he stretched out on
the bed and held her in place when she would have
rolled away. "What? What is it?"

"It happened, didn't it?" she whispered, staring
first at his big hand on her arm, and then into his
eyes. "The bonding thing. It happened."

He scowled at her. "It did, yes. Though it makes
no sense to me."

"You think *that* doesn't make sense?" she countered, tugging free and sliding off the bed before he
could grab her again. "I'm having someone else's
memories. I'm seeing you and me, in another place,
only I'm not me, I'm someone else. And she's—
I'm—running from you. And I don't know what
any of this means, but I can't deal with this now."

She shoved her hair back from her face, took a
deep, shuddering breath and did what she could to
silence the memories still clamoring in her mind.
"I wanted you, I admit that. But I told you going in
that I wasn't interested in being a Mate." Spotting
her clothes lying scattered on the floor, she grabbed
them up and started tugging them on as she talked.

"I have to save my sister. And that's *all* I'm worrying about now."

He sat up, completely at ease in his own nudity. And why wouldn't he be, Alison thought wildly. He looked amazing. Muscles carved into his chest and abdomen. Wide shoulders, long, thick legs and an erection that was already hard and full and ready again.

Standing up, he crossed his arms over his chest, planted his feet wide apart and glared at her as she hurriedly dressed. Oh, it wasn't good that she wanted him again. That the need for him was already rising up and overtaking her again. *Get dressed and get out,* she told herself in a singsong chant.

"We're not Mates," he blurted, catching her attention long enough that she stopped pulling up her jeans.

"I felt it, Rogan. I know you did, too."

"Aye, there was something, I'll admit to that. But it's not that. Cannot be."

"Yeah?" she asked, whipping her hair back over her shoulder. "And how can you know that for sure?"

"Because, blast you, I found my Mate and lost her centuries ago."

Alison staggered, blinked up at him and felt a crushing truth settle on her chest like a hundred-pound weight. "Sinead," she whispered, the name coming into her mind with certainty. Once again, she saw the image of the red-haired, green-eyed woman and she knew the truth in a blinding flash. "Sinead O'Donnel was your Destined Mate."

His features closed up tightly, and fury burned in his eyes. Taking a step closer to her, he grabbed her shoulders and gave her a hard shake. "How do you know this name? Is it your bloody Society? What do they know of Sinead?"

"Nothing," she said as cold seeped into her bones, giving her a soul-deep chill that made every inch of her body shake and tremble with it. Looking into his eyes, she said softly, "The Society knows nothing about her."

"Then how is it you come to know that name?"

"Because I'm her. I'm Sinead O'Donnel. At least," she added, "I used to be."

Chapter 8

The scowl on Rogan's face became even more fierce. "I've no idea what you're about, but this is blather. You're no more Sinead O'Donnel than I am a demon."

Aly glared at him, still shaken by the memories roaring through her mind with the frantic pace of a runaway train. Watching him now, she saw him as he was, here in this sumptuous room—and also how he *had been*, in another time and place. Disconcerting, to say the least.

"From where I'm standing at this moment," she said, "you're sounding like a demon, and how the hell else would I know Sinead's name?"

"Your bloody Society."

The accusation hung in the air. That she'd lied to him. About the Society. About herself. "I've told you she isn't in the files."

He snorted a harsh excuse for a laugh. "And I'm to take your word for that, am I?" Shaking his hair back from his face, he glowered, an ancient, naked warrior, practically vibrating with fury.

"My word's all I've got." Aly zipped up her jeans, slid her feet into her sneakers and thought about kicking him. "Do you think I *want* these memories? Do you think I enjoy remembering some other woman's *life?*"

"How the bloody hell do I know what you want or don't?" he countered and strode across the room without another look at her. Grabbing hold of one of the bookshelves, he tugged at it and it swung open, revealing a well-stocked bar. Quickly, he poured an inch of Irish whiskey into a glass and tossed it down his throat like a punishment. When he'd finished, he speared her with a look again. "You might have arranged all of this for your own purposes."

"Oh, sure. I had my sister kidnapped by a *demon* so I could have sex with you and then stand here defending myself while you look at me like I'm a crazy person!"

"Sex is all I wanted from you."

"Back at you," she snapped. She'd wanted comfort from him. A chance to lose herself for a little while. And instead, she felt as though she might have lost herself permanently. This "connection" with him was strong. It pulled at her to go to him even while she stood her ground stubbornly. Fine, she admitted silently, maybe she had felt more than just a driving need for sex. But damned if she'd admit it now.

Instead, Aly hugged close the hurt his words had caused and pretended she didn't feel a thing. It wasn't easy. With the new and improved connection between them, she could hear his thoughts as easily as her own.

His mind seethed with denial and a carefully banked rage. There was regret, ancient pain and a determination to find answers to what had happened between them.

He poured more whiskey but didn't drink it. Instead, he stared down at the amber liquid as if looking into a crystal ball for answers. "You're not who you say," he murmured, almost to himself. "It can't be so. And even if you were, it changes nothing."

"Why would I lie?"

"Well, now. There's a question."

His calm, rational tone didn't fool her for a minute. The strength of his power simmered in the room. She felt it as it poured over her in thick waves. And yet Aly stood straighter, taller. She wouldn't be held responsible for something she'd had no control over. "I didn't ask for this, you know."

One black eyebrow lifted. "Didn't you?"

"Are you serious?" Insult hummed inside her, wiping away any other emotion. "You *know* why I came here. Why I'm still here."

He slammed the glass of whiskey down on the bar top and spun to face her, accusation flashing in his eyes. "Again, I've only your word to that."

"And the evidence of your own eyes," she countered. "Just because neither one of us wants it to be so, we can't deny what just happened. Your bonding ritual linked us, mind and body. Look into my mind. See for yourself if you don't believe what I'm telling you."

"I'll not."

"Then don't call me a liar just because you're too much a coward to see for yourself that I'm telling the truth."

"A coward, is it?" He bellowed and his voice sounded like thunder, nearly rattling the windowpanes. "I've battled legions of demons for a thousand years." He stomped across the room to stop just in front of her. "I've fought in wars, watched friends die and fulfilled my vow with honor, and you dare to call me a coward?"

Aly supposed he'd be pretty damn intimidating to just about anyone else. But as loud as he shouted, as fierce as he looked, she wasn't afraid of him. In the past couple of days, she'd seen too much, experienced too many frightening, overwhelming things. An angry Guardian was the least of her worries at the moment.

She matched him glare for glare, poked his chest with her index finger and said, "Don't you shout at me. I'm not one of your little demon trolls to be ordered around. You can't tell me what to do, and you are *not* allowed to yell at me."

Then she gave his chest a shove with the flat of her hand, which had as much an effect on him as she'd have found trying to push a mountain to one side. Her heart ached at the dismissal in his eyes. Everything in her yearned for him, and yet he was closing her out. Irritated, she gave in to the urge riding her and kicked his shin. Hard. He didn't even wince.

"No wonder you Guardians have to do the bonding thing. It's the only way you can get a woman to stay with you. Why else would a woman ever put up with the arrogant, bossy, insulting attitudes you ancient warriors throw around?"

"If you're finished," he growled.

"Not yet." She'd keep her feelings for him buried, and since he refused to enter her thoughts, he'd never know that the burning she felt for him was so much stronger than simple sex. He'd never realize that she might have loved him if he'd allowed it. Better that way, she told herself. Better all the way around. She wasn't the Mate kind of woman anyway.

"You keep yourself away from me, you understand? I'm only here until we help Casey. Once my sister is healed, I'm out of here and I never want to see you again."

"At last, we agree on something," he said.

"And, no," she shouted, stepping to the door and opening it, "you *can't* have the last word." Then she slammed the door behind her to prevent it.

"Michael!" Rogan reached for his pants, pulled them on, then said, "Michael, bugger it, show yourself, damn you."

For the first time in too many years to think about, Rogan was shaken. His body throbbed with renewed need for the woman he couldn't trust himself to be around, and the thought of entangling himself with a Destined Mate again was almost more than he could bear.

The last time, it hadn't ended well. Memories of Sinead flowed through him, and in an instant he recalled the agony of losing her with such startling clarity it stole his breath. Now he was faced with what couldn't be. This very modern woman held the memories of his lost love. And more—Alison called to him on the same, gut-deep level as he'd experienced before. If anything, the connection with Alison was stronger, more all-encompassing than the one he'd known with Sinead.

It couldn't be, because the two women couldn't have been more different. Alison knew of his kind. Knew what and who he was. Accepted the very real threat of the demon worlds. Sinead, he thought wearily, remembering her terror, had been a simple peasant girl. One who had no idea what to make of an Immortal or the demons he fought.

He pushed both hands through his hair, tugging at it as he did, as if that minor pain could distract him from the sharper misery within. It didn't help. Every cell in his body hurt. Pain sharp as knives cut at his insides, but Rogan disregarded it. Old pain blended with new into a dizzying combination that made his head pound and his heart squeeze into a cold mass in his chest. And there was no relief in sight.

"Michael!"

Thunder crashed and a blinding flash of light filled the room. Bright white, searing Rogan's eyes until it felt as though needles were being driven into his brain, the light shone brilliantly for a moment, then dimmed to reveal a tall, dark-haired man standing in the middle of the room.

"What is it?" Michael, the being who had first created the Guardians, stared at Rogan through cool eyes that swirled with color, going from blue to green to brown to deep black.

Nearly a thousand years ago, Rogan had died, an enemy's sword through his chest, only to wake up and find this very man standing over him. And in a heartbeat of time, Michael had offered Rogan an eternity of waging war—something he'd proven to have a gift for in life. And Rogan had gladly accepted. He wasn't the one to look for peace in the hereafter. Peace had had no place in his life, and he wouldn't have known what to do with it in death.

And in the centuries since, he'd cut himself off from the humanity he served. He was alone, always—but for once before, nearly five hundred years ago, when he'd loved a woman and lost her.

"That's what I'm asking you," Rogan said, heading for the bar and the drink he'd abandoned. Picking it up, he drank the whiskey down, grateful for the warmth stealing through his veins. He was shaken, something he hadn't wanted Alison to see. Something he hadn't wanted to admit even to himself.

"Sinead O'Donnel."

Michael's eyes darkened in old sympathy. "What about her?"

Rogan looked away from the pity, since it was something he'd no need of. He studied the empty glass, tipping it this way and that, letting the light catch on the fine crystal. "She was my Mate, was she not?"

"She was."

"Then how is it," he asked, slowly turning his head to look at the being he'd known since the moment of his death, so long ago, "I've found another?"

Rogan deliberately set the glass down carefully because his instinct was to hurl it against the wall just to have the satisfaction of seeing it shatter.

Michael sighed, walked toward him, jerked his head at the whiskey and said, "Pour me a short one."

"Oh, aye." Rogan lifted one black brow, but poured the whiskey. As he handed it over, he sneered, "We'll have a drink together, like old friends with no secrets between them. Except there *are* secrets. And I need to know, so tell me."

"Nothing to tell," Michael mused, sipping at the gold liquor and sighing a little with relish. "You've simply found your Mate again."

"*Again?* There is no 'again' so far as I know. There is one Destined Mate for a Guardian, and Sinead is long dead," Rogan reminded him.

Finishing off his whiskey, Michael met Rogan's gaze and said, "And now she's come back."

"Bollocks." He stomped across the room, his big hands clenching and unclenching at his sides. Walking to one of the lead glass pane windows, he threw it open and took a deep, steadying breath of the icy Irish wind. "What the bloody hell does that mean, anyway?"

Michael leaned back against the bookshelves, crossed his feet at the ankles and folded his arms across his chest. "It means that all Guardians have a Destined Mate…"

Rogan shot him a fulminating look over his shoulder. "I bloody well know that, don't I?"

"But there's no guarantee the Guardian will find that Mate."

True enough, Rogan thought. Most of the Guardians he knew were alone in the world. Yet somehow *he'd* managed to do it.

Twice.

"A Mate lives," Michael said quietly, "and if unclaimed by a Guardian, dies and is reborn into the next generation."

Everything in Rogan went still as glass. "Reborn."

"Yes." Michael smiled. "Did you think you were given only one chance to find a Mate, Rogan? Did you believe the Guardians were meant to go through eternity alone?"

He didn't know what to think. He only knew that from the moment he'd first seen Alison Blair, he'd felt something quicken inside him. Something he'd thought long dead. Something he'd thought he'd lost when Sinead died.

"So Alison is—"

"Sinead. Reborn. Just as she has been for centuries. You simply never found her again until now."

With the driving, relentless wind now at his back, Rogan faced the man standing so calmly across the room from him. "And you'd no thought to tell any of us this information?"

"You never asked." Michael smiled and his eyes swirled with color again.

"This is a hell of a trick to play on a man, Michael."

"It's no trick, Rogan," Michael said easily. "It's a gift. To you. To the others like you. The battles you fight, the eternity you live—you're not meant to bear these burdens alone, not meant to suffer for the duty you perform."

"But these Mates are?" Rogan demanded, rage swelling inside him. "Knowing who I am, *what* I am, cost Sinead her life. Do you think I'd willingly live through that again? Put Alison through that? Dear God, *again?* She remembers, you know. And as the memories thicken, will she remember her death? And the fact that it was because of *me* she died?"

"Things are as they're meant to be, Rogan," Michael said and his features stilled; his eyes went black as night and sparked with the lights of thousands of stars, as if he were part of the night himself. "Claim her or not. It's your choice. It always has been."

Then he was gone, in a flash of light as bright as the one he'd arrived in. And Rogan was alone, with a head full of memories and a heart full of pain.

* * *

The next morning Aly stood outside the room where Casey was being kept and listened to the moans and hoarse shrieks drifting through the door. She dropped her head to the door, closed her eyes and tried to find hope within herself.

But to save her sister, she would need Rogan. And how could she face him again after all that had happened the night before? It wasn't only their lovemaking or the awful fight that followed. She'd spent a long, restless night, haunted by dreams of a life lived in a different time and place.

And those images still tumbled through her mind, confused, fractured. *She wore a long skirt, patched at the hem, and a knitted shawl around her shoulders. She had long black hair and kept three tiny silver bells braided into it so that they jingled as she walked, making music with each step.*

She ran to Rogan as he walked into her village and laughed as he swept her up into his arms. He smiled down at her, his eyes filled with a hunger that frightened as well as excited her. His touch was magic, and when she lay beneath him under the stars, she gave herself up to the wonder of it.

Then the images changed and the magic was gone. *There was only fear, her eyes wild with it as Rogan tried to calm her, tried to reach out to her. She turned from him, catching only a glimpse of the pain in his eyes.*

Then she ran, heart pounding in her chest, breath catching in her lungs. The bells in her hair jangled like fury as she pelted headlong down a hill to the safety of the village, hoping, hoping that he wouldn't follow. That he and his tales of demons and eternity would disappear from her mind and heart and leave her in peace.

She'd run from Rogan the moment she'd discovered who and what he was. She hadn't trusted him or herself or the love they shared enough to risk what she feared.

"So who's the coward?" Alison whispered, remembering that only the night before, she'd named him just that, only to find that she herself had been the true coward. She pushed away from the wall, wincing at her sister's shrieks.

The distracting images of a time long dead still swam in her mind, but Alison fought to keep them at bay. That woman, that life, was no more than a shadow from the past. It had nothing to do with the now. With the sister who needed her. With who she herself was today.

She pulled in a deep breath and lifted her head at the sound of heavy footsteps. Turning slowly, she watched Rogan approach with a heavy heart. Strange to look at him and see him through both her own eyes and the eyes of a woman dead these five hundred years.

He looked now as he had then, a warrior. It didn't

matter that today he wore black leather pants and a long-sleeved white shirt. He was the same man who had once worn the colors of his king as he led men into battle. The same man who had stood outside the castle keep and watched as she ran from him, from everything they might have had.

Alison swallowed hard and tasted the bitter dregs of regret. Rogan's gaze as he looked at her was shuttered, revealing nothing of what he might be feeling and maybe, she thought, that was for the best.

Putting whatever lay between she and Rogan to one side, at least for now, Aly said, "I know there are things that we should talk about. But if it's okay by you, I'd rather just concentrate on Casey right now."

Rogan inhaled deeply, blew out the breath in a rush of impatience and said, "I've no interest in speaking about what's between us, Alison. It's in the past and there it'll stay. For now, it's best if we find out what Casey knows."

Not sure whether to be grateful for the reprieve or hurt that he wanted nothing more to do with her, Alison stepped back as he moved forward. Then he put the key in the lock, gave it a turn and opened the door. He walked into the room first, instinctively placing himself between Alison and whatever danger might be waiting.

She peeked around his broad shoulder and felt

everything in her wilt dismally. Her sister, still bound hand and foot, rolled from side to side on the hardwood floor. Her voice was hoarse, but the muttering and shrieking hadn't eased. When her gaze landed on them standing in the doorway, she smiled and her black eyes shone in the morning light streaming through the narrow window.

"The Guardian and his whore," she hissed, spitting the words at them as if they were bullets.

And Aly felt the blow as such.

"That'll be enough of that," Rogan ordered, marching into the room and grabbing Casey off the floor. With little regard for her comfort, he half dragged her to the wall and dropped her into a sitting position, her back against the cold stone. "You've been screaming down my house all the night. So tell us why you're here."

"To kill her." Casey's black gaze landed on Aly, who shivered at the malevolence in that empty stare. Then Casey shifted her gaze to Rogan and gave him a sly smile. "As a warning to you."

"Why? What's your demon up to?" Rogan went down on one knee beside Casey and locked his gaze with hers.

Watching, Aly felt the battle of wills between the Guardian and her sister and knew that Casey would lose. No one could possibly stand against such a powerful man. And almost as she thought it, Casey started speaking again.

Her voice was hard and rough and vicious. Her words were cold but colorful, painting images that were all too real.

"Balam builds an army," Casey said, a proud tilt to her chin.

"Demon armies are nothing new to me, girl."

"His army is made up of those like me," she countered, and Aly saw the glint of triumph lighting her sister's black eyes. "Humans, taken into his dimension, transformed for the glory of Balam."

"Humans can't exist in a demon dimension," Rogan pointed out, and his voice was as calm and still as a lake on a windless day.

"We can and we do. Balam is great. Greater than any you've faced. His army will sweep the world, and he will rule as is only right." She leaned in, her face only a breath away from Rogan's, her eyes bright with madness, her voice a strained whisper. "Those who serve live. Those who don't die. As your woman will die, Guardian."

"Casey…"

Those black eyes turned on Aly, and she almost staggered back at the punch of evil. But she held her ground, looked into her sister's eyes and searched for some trace of the woman she knew. But if Casey was in there, she was buried deep.

"That'll do," Rogan said. Standing up, he dragged Casey back to the middle of the room and left her there, shouting curses and demanding to be freed.

He didn't look back at her, just took a firm grip on Aly's arm and steered her from the room. Once the door was closed and locked again, he stared down at her; Aly read the compassion in his eyes despite the grim slash of his mouth. "Your sister is under a powerful compulsion," he said softly, as if he wished he didn't have to say these things but knew he had no choice. "There may be no getting her back."

"I can't accept that," Aly said, meeting his gaze. "I won't accept it. Rogan, whatever is between us…"

He dropped her arm as if burned, but she kept talking, not willing to let him turn his back until she'd said what she felt she had to.

"…Casey's my sister. I'm going to do everything I can to free her from this damn demon. But I can't do it alone. I'll need you. Your help. Your strength. Your knowledge. You're my only hope, and therefore Casey's only hope, too."

His eyes narrowed and his features tightened. "I've given my word to do what I can, and so I will. But as to the other, what lies between us," he added, "that's long over. And I'll not be a party to reawakening it, no matter the bonding."

She nodded, because how could she blame him for shutting her out? Hadn't she done the same thing to him hundreds of years ago? The jagged pieces of her memory were still a tumble, like a jigsaw puzzle that had been dumped on a tabletop. A tangle of disconnected shards that showed only glimpses of the real picture, only tantalizing portions of the whole.

Yet, she knew enough to be aware of what the woman she had once been had done.

She'd turned her back on his offer of love and then had died before she could change her mind.

Chapter 9

Rogan fought the instinct to hold her close and told himself it was for both of them that he did it. They'd both lost centuries ago, and he saw no reason to fight the same war again.

Sinead or Alison, the soul remained the same. Reborn into a new time, with a different life and different feelings, she was still, at the bottom of it, a woman who had torn his heart from his chest.

Erecting mental barriers against her, he stood tall and alone. He'd once let a woman close enough to him to devastate him. He wouldn't make that mistake again. How could he trust she wouldn't do the same thing she'd done so long ago?

"What's done is done," he said solemnly. "There's no going back to undo it. Not today, not then."

"Rogan, I don't understand half of what's happening to me." She sighed, folded her arms over her chest, then unfolded them, moving nervously as if she didn't know what to do with herself. A part of him wanted to comfort her, ease the confusion in her eyes and the sorrow in her voice.

But to do that would only be to invite disaster. And hadn't they enough trouble as it stood already?

"Doesn't matter," he told her and waited until she looked him in the eye. He knew then that he would always remember the blue of her eyes, even if he never saw her again. For decades, he'd dreamed of Sinead, heard her laughter, felt her warmth.

And what he'd felt for her was but a shadow of what he was coming to feel for Alison. Destined Mate or no, it seemed that he and this woman were far more attuned than he and Sinead had ever been. Which only made it more imperative for him to block her from his mind and his heart.

To give himself to this woman and to lose her would mean centuries of pain. Which he'd no desire to endure.

"We'll leave it lie," he said quietly. "Let the past stay buried as it should and keep from making the same mistakes again."

She nodded, but the pain was still in her eyes,

and he knew it would be harder for her to do as he'd said. After all, his memories of Sinead were centuries old. For Alison they were fresh and new and filled with bright pain, undimmed by the years.

She rubbed her forehead as if trying to ease an ache she couldn't name, and Rogan, to distract her, spoke briskly. "This demon's a different matter altogether. If it's found a way to turn mortals, then we'd best find out all we can about it."

Alison drew in a deep breath and asked, "How do we do that exactly?"

Frowning, he turned for the stairs and listened to her quick footsteps as she followed. "You should go to Dublin. To the Society there. Surely there's mention somewhere in your bloody damn files about a demon trying this before."

Plus, it would get her out of the house and give them both some desperately needed breathing room.

"I'll look," she said but sounded doubtful. "What're you going to do?"

At the foot of the stairs, he drew her into the library and waved her into a chair. "I'm going hunting. I'll start in Westport near where Casey was taken. If this demon Balam's after building an army, I'm thinking there'll be more demons looking for other recruits."

The light in the room dimmed as clouds skittered across the sky, obliterating the sun. Through the window, he watched as the wind tore at trees, glee-fully snatching new leaves and tossing them into the air. On the lake, whitecaps frothed, churned by that same wind, and birds swooped out of the sky, look-ing for a safe harbor.

But safe harbors were hard to find, as well Rogan knew. He'd thought he'd found one here, at Lough Mask. He'd buried himself in the country he loved, within sight of the ruined keep that had haunted him always. Best, he'd thought, then and now, to stay close to the keep, where he wouldn't be tempted to forget the misery that came with loving and losing. And he'd hunted demons because he'd vowed to do so and because fighting was all he knew. He'd lost himself in time and thought to put Sinead and all that might have been behind him.

Yet here she was again.

Tempting him to believe.

He shook his head, spared Alison a brief glance and said, "Sean will drive you into the city. And while you're there," he said, a thought occurring to him, "see what you can find on a group known as the Acolytes."

Her head lifted and her gaze bored into his. "I've heard of them. Weren't they involved in a sacrifice for a demon thirty years ago?"

"They were, yes. But they're busy now as well. Just a few months ago another Guardian had dealings with the fringes of them and those who oppose them."

"Santos," she whispered and Rogan smiled.

"Aye. Santos and his Mate were drawn into a web spun by Abbadon."

"I remember reading about this just before I came here. Wasn't Santos's Mate Abbadon's daughter?"

"She is."

"And they found a way to bring her back from the demon world," Alison said, her voice colored by a hope she needed to cling to.

Rogan didn't want to snatch that hope from her, but better to know the truth than not. "It was different, Alison. Erin hadn't been turned. She was still human when her demon father did all he could to kill her."

"Casey's human, too," she protested.

"Aye, her body. But her mind's been turned, and we've no way of knowing if it can be reversed."

She pushed up out of the chair as if she couldn't bear to sit still another moment. Walking across the room, she stared out the window at the gray world beyond and said, "We don't know that it can't, either."

"True. And we'll do all we can for her. That's why you must go to Dublin. Gather information."

"I'll go," she said and slowly turned to look at him.

The strength of her gaze punched at him, and

desire hit him even harder than it had the night before. He wanted her with a hunger that was fierce enough to make him tremble from it. And Rogan knew he couldn't have her—not if he was to give her up. And he *would* give her up.

The tick of a clock sounded loud in the room, like a steadier heartbeat than either of them could claim at the moment. Rogan watched her as she gathered her strength and wrapped it around her like a shield.

"I'll go to Dublin," she repeated. "I'll find what I can. But, Rogan, ignoring what's between us doesn't change anything. Doesn't fix anything."

"Some things," he said, "when broken, can't be put together again, Alison. A wise man knows enough to recognize it."

At any other time, Alison would have loved being in the Society headquarters in Dublin. Built of gray stone, now weathered, the building had been in the same spot for more than four hundred years. It stood on the fringes of Phoenix Park, on the outskirts of the city itself.

Situated on North Road, past the Dublin Zoo and the huge fish pond, the building stood alone in a stand of trees. It had been there so long it was as if it had become a part of the scenery. A small brass plaque on the gate in front of the building identified it as being a private library, so the Society wouldn't be bothered by civilians wandering in.

The main room was a tremendous space, three stories tall; the walls were covered with bookshelves that stretched to the ceiling. There were wide landings on the second and third floors that wrapped around the interior of the room and offered tables, chairs and ladders on tracks to help gather up whatever research books were needed. The room smelled of lemon polish, leather and musty books. To someone such as Aly, it was as close to heaven as a person could find. Only a handful of people had come and gone in the two days Aly had spent at the library, and the silence was deafening.

Outside the leaded windows, rain spat at the building and hammered the city. There was a fire and plenty of lamplight, but Aly felt as though she were suffocating in darkness anyway. She hadn't seen Rogan since the morning after their night together. She hadn't felt his mind in hers, hadn't caught the barest whisper of his voice.

And she'd never felt more alone.

Her chest felt heavy, and her eyes were always on the brink of tears. She'd lost her sister, and now she'd lost the connection she'd found so briefly, with Rogan. And the pain of those losses pounded into her night and day.

Her dreams were filled with images of a life she could remember only in sleep. And her waking hours were spent here, hovering over ancient books, locked away from everything she cared about. The worst part of it was that she'd found nothing in her search. No mention of demons building human armies. No hint as to how a human might survive in a demon dimension. And no reports of the Acolytes being part of whatever was happening at the moment.

Though she *had* found something that had nothing to do with the problem at hand and everything to do with the past. In a five-hundred-year-old manuscript, she'd found mention of Sinead O'Donnel and the Guardian Rogan Butler.

Seeing it in writing had somehow made the dreams and the memories all the more real. She'd lost herself in the words scrawled on the fragile pages and had suffered anew as even more images filled her mind.

So all she had to show for two days of work was more pain.

"God, this is useless," she whispered, sitting back in her chair. Scraping one hand over her hair, she pushed it behind her ears and stared blindly down at the open book in front of her. It was only one of a hundred like it she'd examined in the past two days. And it was one more dead end.

"You've found nothing, then?"

The quiet, gentle voice startled her, and Aly looked up into a familiar face. The Society administrator, Garret O'Reilly, was at least eighty, with sparse white hair, sharp green eyes and a ready smile.

"Nothing yet," she admitted and felt the quick jolt of failure snap at her insides. "Are you sure there's no mention anywhere of a demon trying to build a human army?"

He shook his head and sighed as his gnarled fingers tugged and smoothed his bright red tie. "I've thought and thought, even called in a favor or two and spoke to my counterparts in Rome and Sydney. But no one's heard of anything like this. It's a worry, I'll admit to you. If the demon world's found a way to turn a mortal, this could tip the tide in their favor."

"I know." And that knowledge settled like a shroud over her.

"Santino," Garret mused, "my friend in Rome, suggested that perhaps the Guardian Romulus might know of something."

Aly sat up a bit straighter. Romulus was the oldest of the Guardians, said to have existed since before the birth of Christ. It only made sense that if anything like this had happened before, the ancient warrior would have heard of it.

"But," Aly said, even as eagerness pitched into life inside her, "Romulus speaks to no one. Even the other Guardians give him a wide berth."

"True," Garret said, giving her a quick smile. "He's a wily one, all right. But we've some of the journals related to Romulus here at the library."

"They're here? Not in Rome?"

Garret crooked a finger at her, to indicate she should follow him, and then started off across the glossy, inlaid wood floor. His shoes smacked briskly with every step, and the sound echoed in the cavernous chamber. Aly hurried after him.

"I've got them on loan. They arrived only a month or so ago, and I've not had the chance to read them in depth." He glanced over his shoulder at her. "Perhaps you'll find something to aid you there."

Hope lifted inside her, and Aly clung to it like it was a life preserver. And it very well might. If they couldn't find a way to defeat this demon Balam, then the entire human world was at risk. Not just the sister she loved.

When Garret left her in a small, windowless room, with the precious journals laid out on a desk, she closed her mind to everything but the niggling hope that she still might find a way out of this.

For two days Rogan had stalked the streets of Westport, invisible to all he passed. It was the only way. The rage that crouched inside him burned through every pore in his body, and he knew that if the citizens of this city could see him, they'd scatter like ants from the scent of danger emanating from him.

His mind seethed with every step, and the only

relief he experienced came when he found a demon. Three now he'd dispatched this day alone, and for him that was a record of sorts. But there was no time for pride—because the very presence of so many demons at once told him that Casey's corruptor, Balam, was, as she'd said, busily making inroads into the mortal world.

And that knowledge fed the fury within. That a demon would attempt to build his army on the land Rogan had sworn to protect and defend cut deep. He'd rid the world of this damned threat and return Alison's sister to her. Then she would leave Ireland and he could begin to forget. Again.

He'd survived Sinead. He would survive this as well.

He was immortal and would accept nothing less.

Forcing his mind from thoughts of Alison, he fought the urge to mentally call to her. To slip into her mind. But those small connections only fed the larger ones and would make the chains binding them that much harder to break.

He'd avoided her for the past two days, keeping himself away from his home. Casey was safe enough, bound in the tower room. Sean was driving Alison to and from Dublin City. Maggie was the one Alison talked with in the evening. And though he'd stopped outside Alison's bedroom door to listen for a sound from her, he hadn't gone to her, hadn't called her to him.

The ache of wanting her was driving him to madness, but he didn't surrender to it. The wanting would fade. In time. And God knew, he had centuries of time.

Focusing again on the hunt, he caught snatches of conversations, bits of laughter and the scent of steak and kidney pie drifting through the open door of a pub. Small lives clicking forward, with no thought to what lay just beyond their knowing. He couldn't be everywhere at once, and as Rogan looked about him at the people streaming along the sidewalks, driving down the roads, he knew that somewhere amid all of this life, demons lurked.

Overhead, seagulls wheeled and screeched against a gunmetal-gray sky. The sun was setting; Rogan felt its slide from the heavens down to his bones. But the storm rolling in off the sea hid everything in a thick mist that became fat drops of rain spattering to earth. Thunder rolled and a brief flash of lightning illuminated the clouds.

All around him people scuttled for doorways, but Rogan kept moving through the wet. What did he care about a sudden storm? If anything, the weather would keep the streets clear of mortals, making the demons edgier, less careful. With fewer humans to choose from, the demons would be more eager to catch hold of those who might not seek shelter.

Gaze narrowed, jaw tight, Rogan loped down the wide avenue, slipping around a corner to stride along the river walk. Here was where Casey was taken, and here there might be any number of demons hiding, waiting for a chance to snatch an unwary human. Hadn't he caught one just last night, trying to burrow into the ground just as Rogan's net fell over it? Eyes primed to catch any sense of demon energy left behind, Rogan put Alison firmly out of his mind and concentrated on what he did best.

What he needed was another fight. A full-out, fists-and-knives, battle-to-the-death fight. The three demons he'd fought already this day had barely taken the edge off. He needed more. He craved the rush of battle, the losing of himself in the breathless clash of enemies coming together. And when he spotted a twisting strand of faded purple flying in the wind like a limp battle flag, he chased it down like a hound on a fox.

He bolted down an alley that smelled of old beer and trash. The ground was littered with garbage, and the stench got heavier the farther he went into the deepening shadows. The brick buildings on either side of the alley were steep and windowless, so no light shone here. Rogan felt alert, ready. Embracing the darkness because it was there that he was most at home.

Another swirl of purple stood out in the dimness, and Rogan felt a roaring need for combat rise up inside him. He bent low and pulled a dagger from his boot. A sword would be quicker, but he was in a mind to hurt something. Might as well be this demon as another.

A scratch of sound jarred him, and he spun around in time to swing one arm up and slice the demon across the chest as it lunged at him. A howl of pain pierced his ears and brought a grim smile from Rogan.

Here, then, was where he belonged.

Rain quickened and the thunder rattled the air. Lightning flashed again, illuminating the alley that was as dark as the pit of hell. Still screaming like a banshee, the demon landed hard, slammed into the wall and leaped away an instant later. Red eyes flickered in the light, a wide, gaping jaw displayed sharp teeth an inch or more in length and the claws at the tips of its fingers were daggerlike.

With a hiss it swept out one long arm and caught Rogan's side with one of those lethal claws. Pain slashed across his side, and he felt the burn slide deep within. Yet it only fed the rage pumping inside as he ran at the creature shifting from foot to foot in eager anticipation. Fool that it was, it didn't fear what was coming. Mindless creatures, most of them, demons knew only blood and pain and had no thought at all of self-preservation.

Rogan could have told it that was a mistake.

He charged it, with a battle cry howling from his throat. The demon sucked in air and looked for an escape route that didn't exist. There was nowhere to run and Rogan wouldn't be denied.

He hit the demon firmly in the midsection, throwing it back into the wall. It hit hard, then slid down to land in the trash. A beer bottle dislodged by the fall skittered across the alley and shattered against the far wall. Stunned, the demon shook its head.

"You're hunting my streets, demon," Rogan said, coming in low with the dagger. "And you'll not be doing it again anytime soon."

Rogan plunged the dagger through the demon's chest and felt only satisfaction as the damn thing twisted and squirmed, trying to peel itself free. Though the demons couldn't be killed easily in this dimension, they could be wounded badly enough that it would take them some time to recover before attempting another incursion.

And that was all Rogan could ask for. Disgust curled his lips as he stared down at the demon while grabbing for the Guardian net he carried in his pocket. "You were a poor hunt, demon."

It laughed, tugging at the dagger in its chest. "Ah, Guardian," it cooed, eyes flashing in the dark alley, "I'm not the one you should be hunting. There's another, and when he comes, you'll be the one on the wrong end of a blade."

Rogan frowned at it and whipped his long hair back behind his shoulder. "I've heard threats from your kind before. It's no matter to me. I'm still standing, aren't I?"

He dropped the net over the demon, and instantly the damn thing came alive with jumping and rolling and twisting, trying to escape though it had to know the effort was futile. "Still standing now, Guardian, but soon to fall. As will you all. Fall, fall, down into the dark, where we will rule and you will die."

Rogan went down on one knee in the muck and peered into those red eyes. "If you've something to say, demon, say it. Otherwise shut that howling hole in your face before I close it up tight for you."

Caught in the net, the creature went suddenly still as death. It blinked those fiery eyes, then smiled wickedly, teeth glinting in the flash of the lightning overhead.

"The army grows," it murmured, clearly unable to keep quiet for longer than a breath at a stretch. "The king awaits. And your kind will soon serve us."

The army.

Did this demon know about Balam? Or was it, as was more likely, only repeating what it had heard in its own dimension?

"More demon swill," Rogan said, spitting the words as he yanked his dagger free of the demon, wiped off the black blood on the creature's own body and slid the knife back into its scabbard.

"You wish it were so," the demon said, talking as Rogan had hoped it would. "But my master comes. He takes your kind and returns them to you more us than you, and when they return to him, they come not alone."

"Poetry now, is it?" Rogan asked with a shake of his head. "You're talking in riddles, creature, and I've no time to play your games. If you do have a king, mind you tell him when you get back to where you came from, that Rogan Butler stands on Ireland, and I'll keep him and his kind from this world with my last breath."

The demon licked Rogan's blood from its claw with a long, pointed tongue, shivered as if enjoying the flavor, then pointed that claw at him. "Your last breath, Guardian, is just what my master wants."

A grim, satisfied smile curved Rogan's mouth. It seemed he'd finally found a demon who might actually know something. Leaning in, he ignored the stench of the beast as he sighed, "Well, then, demon, if you've a need to talk, I've a mind to listen. Tell me, then, just what sort of mischief is it your master has planned?"

Too late; the demon realized that it had talked its way into trouble. Its gaze flicked back and forth, checking the shadows surrounding it as if looking for allies that weren't there.

"Ah," Rogan said, "there you are, then. Noticed it's just you and me here, have you, demon? Where's your pride, you bloody creature? If you're so sure of your king, as you claim, surely you'll want to boast about his plans. And the sooner you tell me what you know, the sooner I shove you back into your hell."

The demon pulled its head back, cringing into itself, yet in its eyes, Rogan read resignation. Pleased, he prepared for an interrogation.

Rogan...

Blast it all to hell and back again. She was here with him, in the stinking alley. Just the sigh of her voice was enough to dredge up the taste of her, the scent of her, the feel of her beneath his hands.

He lifted his head, staring off into the thunderous skies as Alison's voice rushed into his mind. He didn't want to answer her. Didn't want to even acknowledge the fact that just that swift, brief connection to her had his body tightening and his heartbeat quickening into a gallop.

Rogan, I think I found something.

He felt her excitement and realized that their mental bond, strengthened by their lovemaking, had solidified into something more powerful than anything he'd ever known before. He could hear the beat of her heart, feel a thrill of anticipation shooting through her—and more, he felt the warmth of her, sliding deep within him.

Steeling himself, he frowned at his captive and opened himself to Alison. *What have you found?*

Oh, thank God. I thought you weren't going to answer me.

I've a captive demon to deal with Alison. If you've something to tell me, say it and be done.

There was a long silence, and he knew she was hurt by his tone. But he had no time for niceties.

I read something in the journals on Romulus. In 450, a demon called Talon used a fruit grown in his dimension to gain control of humans.

Fruit? He nearly laughed aloud at the ridiculousness of it. But on the off chance that this was true, he speared his captive with a dangerous look and asked, "What do you know of a fruit in the demon dimensions? One used against mortals."

The creature didn't answer him.

It didn't have to.

The truth was written plainly on its scarred face. Its eyes went wide, its mouth was closed and flattened and it looked as though it wished it were anywhere but there.

You're onto something, Alison, Rogan told her, sending his thoughts and the sense of satisfaction he felt hurtling toward her. *The demon I've captured knows of this fruit. Find out what you can and I'll see you at home.*

Soon, she whispered.

And when their connection was severed, Rogan felt the yawning emptiness that had been the staple of his life reach up to swallow him again.

Chapter 10

At the castle Rogan waited for Alison, impatience pushing at him. He felt the sting of the demon burn still tugging at his flesh, but the salve he'd applied would soon take care of that minor irritation. His insides felt jumpy and his gaze kept flashing to the front door, as if continually checking for her would make her suddenly appear.

Shoving one hand through his long hair, he muttered a curse in Gaelic. Didn't seem to matter that he knew he would soon be letting her go, that he *wanted* to let her go, his body, his brain, his soul needed her here. And the thought of spending the rest of eternity looking at that front door in futile hope filled him with a marrow-deep sorrow that threatened to buckle his legs.

"Where the hell is she?" he asked of no one. The drive from Dublin was a long one, at least two hours, but it seemed as though he'd been waiting for centuries.

And so he had, he thought grimly.

When the front door flew open, his heart jolted in his chest and his gaze locked on the slice of night pouring into the house. He didn't breathe. Didn't move. And there she was, her long blond hair wind-blown, her cheeks flushed from the kiss of the wind and her eyes turning to him. For just a moment he did nothing but look at her.

The house felt whole again with her presence. It was as if even the air itself had been charged. He felt the pull of instincts as old as time drawing him to her and had to force himself to stand still. He wanted her more than he'd ever wanted anything, and yet he knew that to go to her now would only make her leaving that much harder to bear. He'd lived hundreds of years without her in his life. He could and would do it again. Pain would be his companion over the coming eternity—but then pain and he had long been acquainted.

She slipped out of her jacket as she walked into the room, and Rogan's gaze swept over her hungrily. Her jeans were faded and clung to her legs. The long-sleeved green shirt she wore was unbuttoned at the throat, and her silver necklace shone in the lamplight. Her eyes were wary, but the gleam of excitement was there as well. Her breathing was steady and her steps were measured as she came toward him.

Her scent filled the room and him as well as he took a long, deep breath, deliberately capturing her scent, holding it within. He'd hoped that small taste of her would ease the tension coiled at the base of his spine. But instead, he felt that tension ratchet up another few notches.

"Did you return the demon to its dimension?"

"What?" He shook his head and backed up a step until he was standing before the fire in the hearth. Heat poured from the dancing flames and licked at the backs of his legs. Yet still, Rogan felt cold, colder than he had been in years. Rubbing one hand across his jaw, he spoke again, hoping to ease the strained silence sizzling in the air between them. "I didn't, no. For now, it's locked up in the basement. It's in the Guardian netting, so it won't be getting loose, though."

"Did it tell you anything?" she asked.

"Nothing we didn't already know," he said, disgusted with the creature's descent into whining pleas for mercy. "I kept it here because I don't want the little toad to go back and give a warning to the others. I did take it to the portal and held it there until the portal opened, so I know which dimension we want."

"Good," she said and licked her lips nervously. "That's good."

He fought back the pounding beat of desire clamoring in his head, kept his mental barriers erected so she wouldn't feel what he didn't want her to feel, and said, "After, I tried to phone Rom."

Her eyes widened. "Romulus?"

"He wasn't there," Rogan said, frowning. "His housekeeper told me he's been off for weeks. She's no idea where he is."

Alison sighed and rubbed her hands up and down her arms as though she felt the cold as deeply as he. "So no help from that quarter."

"No," Rogan admitted and the sting of defeat snapped at him. "But when I couldn't reach Rom, I called Karras."

Now she looked at him in stunned disbelief. "Karras? Isn't he…"

He didn't need a peek into her mind to tell him what she was thinking now. It was clear on her face. The Society poked its collective noses into the lives and works of the Guardians, but even at that, there remained secrets. Secrets shared only between those who lived the eternal life of warriors. They protected their own as well as humankind. But these were special times, and if truth be known, Alison was special herself. So he gave her the truth that had only been hinted at for the past few hundred years. "Aye. It's true, though you're not to write this down in one of your blasted Society journals."

"I understand," she whispered, her voice nearly lost in the sigh of the wind across the top of the chimney.

He nodded, accepting her word because he knew she valued it. "Karras is what you've heard. A werewolf."

She staggered back a step or two and shook her head in disbelief. "A Guardian werewolf."

"His change came before he was made a Guardian, and so when given eternity, that change remained." Rogan scowled now, thinking of how his friend had borne the misery of becoming a monster every month because his honor had demanded he accept the role of immortal Guardian. "He's a good man. A good friend."

"I understand," Alison said, meeting his gaze. "I won't say anything."

"That's good, then," Rogan continued, half listening to the rain pelting the windows and the snap and crackle of the flames. "When Karras was first made a Guardian, he trained with Rom. If anyone besides the oldest one would know anything, it would be Karras."

"Did he?"

"We'll get to that. First, tell me what you found."

She looked at him for a long minute, as if she were trying to read him. Then she gave it up and instead of moving closer to him, she dropped into a chair and tucked her legs up beneath her. Rogan drew his first easy breath since she'd entered the room. In that chair, she wouldn't be coming closer to him. And he would not allow himself to go to her.

Scooping her hair back from her face, she let her head fall against the chair. She took a breath as if bracing herself and said, "According to the journal, this fruit, once eaten by humans, either will allow them to live in the demon dimensions—turning them somehow—or will kill them instantly."

The pain in her voice called to him. The despair of it ate at him. And there was nothing he could do to ease it. Her fears were a living thing in the dimly lit room, and they grew teeth and snarled as the seconds ticked past.

Finally, he gave her the only thing he could by reminding her, "Casey's alive."

When she lifted her head to him again, there were tears in her eyes that tore at Rogan with the vicious swipe of a dagger. "Yes. She must have eaten the fruit. She survived, but..." She swallowed hard, lifted her chin and said, "Balam must be using the fruit to build his army."

Her strength humbled him. He looked at her quiet suffering, and her determination to remain steadfast filled him with admiration for her. She was a woman of honor. Of power. Her terror was real and sharp, tearing at her. But she would never let her fears stop her from going after whatever it was she wanted.

She wasn't Sinead.

But as that name slid through his mind, Rogan felt cold steal over him. And as if she were finely attuned to his every sense, she spoke.

"While I was at the library, I found other journals. They mentioned you. And…her."

His gaze narrowed and a strange heat filled him quickly, replacing the cold with the dark fire of betrayal. Anger. "You said she wasn't mentioned in the Society archives."

"Not in Chicago, no." She said it quickly, as if guessing that he was thinking she'd lied to him. "But here, in Ireland, where it all happened…" She pulled in a breath, wrapped her arms around her legs and looked up at him, sorrow and regret shining in her eyes. "I know what happened."

His features went hard as stone. He felt himself withdraw from the room, from her, though he hadn't moved a muscle. "Reading a few lines scribbled on a page by some nameless scribe tells you nothing."

"Fine, then," she said and, shifting, pushed herself out of the chair. She moved slowly, as if every bone in her body ached. As if weariness dragged at her, and a part of him wanted to gather her close and take her to bed. But that would solve nothing.

"I read the journals, and they were as you thought, just dry facts, scrawled across a page with little care. But the words aren't what made me know. Reading them, seeing them, there on the faded pieces of manuscript, I remembered." She stared at him, her gaze meeting his, boring into his as if daring him to challenge her—and how could he? Rogan could see the truth on her face, could feel it in the waves of pain that rushed from her in surge after surge.

"I remembered so much, Rogan." She shook her head, turned her back on him and walked to the window across the room. She stared at the glass and the night beyond as if she couldn't bear to meet his gaze any longer. He didn't know whether to be pleased or saddened by that fact.

He looked into her mind, unable to help himself, and the desolation he found there was soul deep. A terrifying emptiness that seemed to blossom and grow, a spreading blackness sliding through her body.

Rain beat at the glass like tiny fists. Lightning shimmered behind a low bank of clouds and sent pale shadows dancing across the surface of the lake that lay black in the night. And still she stared, silent, watchful. Was she here with him now, or was she looking into a past she'd only just discovered?

He felt her pain and didn't want it. Didn't want

to bear it for her or know that she suffered it. Fisting his hands at his sides, he retreated from her mind and said, "That time's long past, Alison."

"It's not." She whispered the words, but they resonated in the room with an urgency he couldn't deny. Glancing back over her shoulder at him, she said, "It's here with us now. In this room. It's on your face and in my heart." Her lips twisted and her eyes filled. "I was wrong, Rogan."

"Don't." One word, an order to be obeyed, and yet she was oblivious.

"I was wrong to run from you," she said, then turned to look back at the night again, as if she could find the peace she was searching for out there somewhere, in the shadows.

"We'll not do this, Alison," he said and took a step toward her before catching himself and forcing his body to stop. If he touched her now, one or both of them would shatter. And he wouldn't have it. "Whatever game the Fates are playing with us, we won't oblige them. This was—" He caught his breath, blew it out. "This was done. *We* were done long ago."

"It's never finished," she whispered, her voice hardly more than a breath. "Not while so much is left unsaid." She lifted one hand and laid it on the glass as if trying to feel the cool slide of the rain against her palm. "So I'll say it now as it should have been said then. I was *wrong*. Or *she* was. It was me, but not, and I know that doesn't make sense, but does any of this?"

Her mind called out to his, and he could do nothing but answer her. Instinct drove where reason held back. Mentally he offered her comfort, and aloud he said, "Alison, there's no point to this."

"I feel your touch in my mind, so you know, you *feel,* that there is a point to this." Her voice became louder, steadier, as if she were bringing to bear the last of her strength. "My sister's upstairs practically foaming at the mouth. Some demon leader is planning to take over the world. And I'm the reincarnation of a woman who died five hundred years ago! None of this is rational. None of this should be happening. But it is. And I have to tell you," she said, whirling around now, facing him with the soft lamplight shining on her like a blessing. "You told me—her—Sinead that you loved her. She loved you, too. You know that, right?"

There would be no escape then, Rogan thought and braced himself to have it over and done. Setting his feet wide apart, he crossed his arms over his chest and gave her a glare that had been known to send demons cringing in terror. She only looked at him, waiting. "Aye, I know she loved me. But it wasn't enough."

"No," she agreed, and her voice carried the weight of the tears coursing down her cheeks like drops of crystal. "It wasn't enough because she was afraid."

"Of *what?*" His voice thundered in the room, clashing with the roll and crash of the heavens outside. Frustrations that had nibbled on him for five hundred years were suddenly released into the room. "I would have protected her. She'd nothing to fear from me and well you know it."

"She saw you, fighting a demon."

The air left him in a rush. "Ah, sweet mother…"

"She sneaked out of the keep one night and went to you, but there was a portal near the lake and she saw you." Alison drew a breath and kept talking, the words tumbling from her mouth, one after the other as if in a race to get it all said at long last. "She saw the creature you fought and she saw you send it back through the open portal, and it terrified her."

"She didn't tell me."

"She couldn't. I couldn't. When you came to her—me—you told her—me—" Shaking her head again, Alison whispered, "This is giving me a headache."

He crossed the room to her, unwilling to stay apart now when the gates between them had been flung wide. He'd fought this, but now he would have it all out in the open between them at last. He would finish this, and then when they parted, they would go clean.

Taking her shoulders in his big hands, Rogan pulled her in toward him until she lifted her face to his, meeting his gaze. "I told her about my immortality. I offered to find a way to make her immortal as well. To love her forever."

"And she—I—was scared, Rogan."

"You'd nothing to fear from me." He repeated the words as if he had to make her at least admit that much to him.

"I know that. Knew it then, too. But she— Screw it. *We* were more terrified of what you were than what you fought. The thought of living forever seemed like witchcraft. Dark magic. Loving you wasn't enough. We ran because we couldn't love a man in league with the devil."

He stared at her, furious but strangely calm, as well. As if a blanket of rationality had been draped over the rage, smothering, but not extinguishing it. "The devil. That's not what you ran from. Oh, that's what you tell yourself, then and now. But the truth of it is, you couldn't face your own fears of leaving your home, your family, for *me*. You told yourself that I was the devil, because then you could stay locked in your safe little world. But it didn't turn out to be so safe, did it, Alison?"

"No." She pulled away from him, and he felt the loss of her down to the bone. "It didn't."

"And do you know why?"

"A demon came."

"Aye. A demon, a demon a seer told me had gone from there. A demon I chased into the Burren, taking the seer's vision as truth. And when I came back," he said, feeling the old pain, the old fury rise up again and chew at him, "empty-handed—for there'd been no demon where the seer sent me—the village was gone. Destroyed. Burned to the ground. And you and all your family were dead."

"I know…" She trembled, wrapped her arms around her middle and looked anywhere but at him.

"Aye, you read it in your blasted Society papers," he ground out. "But what you don't know is that I knelt there in the ashes and held your broken body for three days. I wept like a child, bereft of all hope with an eternity of emptiness stretching out in front of me. I couldn't let you go, you see, even though you'd turned from me. And when I buried you, I buried all I felt for you as well. I won't go down this road again with you, Alison."

"I'm not her."

"Aye," he said, feeling the cold wash back into him, and taking it for strength, holding it close, wrapping his heart in the icy grip that would keep him strong. "But you once were and your soul is the same as the one who left me broken. The same as the one who died rather than love me."

Casey shrieked and howled and spat out the food Aly tried to give her. Though her voice was broken from screaming, the madness kept a grip on her, holding her captive as surely as a Guardian net would have.

Aly sat across from her sister and hugged her knees to her chest. She felt as though she'd been fighting a battle for days. Weeks. Her heart ached and her body felt as empty as the curses pouring from Casey's mouth.

Rogan was gone, out to search the portal for what he could find of the demon's plans. And Aly could do nothing but sit here and wait. Sit here and mourn for what had once been, for what might have been.

Casey rolled across the floor, her bonds preventing her from hurting herself as she continued to writhe in need for a master that had infiltrated her soul.

Aly was alone. Truly alone. The memories of losing Rogan five hundred years ago were so fresh in her mind now that it could have happened yesterday. She remembered it all so clearly.

The panic, knowing, believing, that Rogan was truly immortal. He would never know heaven or hell. He would simply go on, through time. And when he offered the same to her, Aly/Sinead could only weep, terrified at the thought of losing all she knew, all she'd ever known, for the love of a single man.

She looked up at him, his green eyes shining in his sharply chiseled face, and she made the sign of the cross. The mark to protect her against devilry. And with him shouting her name, she ran. Back to the village. Back to her family. Closing him out of her mind, her heart, and willing herself to forget.

She hadn't, though. Hadn't forgotten. Hadn't stopped wanting. And when the demon came and killed her with one swipe of a jagged nail across her throat, her last thought had been for Rogan and what she'd lost.

Alison angrily brushed the tears from her cheeks. Useless—the tears were useless. Crying for a decision made too long ago to change. But the tears were for her in the here and now, too, and even knowing that didn't make her crying more helpful. Unbelievably tired, she rested her head against the stone wall behind her. "He was right about one thing. It's over and done and nothing can change what was."

"You'll die," Casey crooned, her hoarse voice dropping to a notch just above a scratch. "You'll all die."

And maybe they would, Alison thought. After their heartbreaking discussion about the past, Rogan had shut off his emotions and told her all that he'd learned from Karras. There was only one way to stop this demon's threat. The way Romulus had ended things more than a thousand years ago.

The ancient Guardian had gone to the demon dimension himself to face Talon. And in its own world, the demon had died—and with it its plans for dominion over humanity.

But watching her sister, Aly worried. If the demon was killed before Casey was released from its hold, what would happen to her? Would she be trapped in this half-world forever, her mind lost to a demon, her life destroyed for a lost cause?

No. Aly wouldn't let that happen. With or without Rogan's help, she would find the way to bring her sister back from the hell she was caught in.

With his sword gripped in his right hand and a dagger in his left, Rogan stood before the portal. Here, at the foot of the hill from the keep, beside the now-glassy waters of the lake, the opening into other dimensions lay hidden until opened by either a demon or a Guardian.

Above his head the sky was clear, the last of the clouds blowing out to sea. Stars shone brilliantly in the freshly washed heavens, and the wind for once was silent. A night bird called for its mate, and the sigh of the water moving to shore was a whisper of sound.

Behind every tree and bush lay deeper shadows, blacker spots in the night, and he reached out with his senses to examine every one. Keeping Alison from his mind, he gave himself up to the moment at hand. She wasn't a part of this. And thoughts of a woman had no place here.

Lifting his head, he forced open the dimensional

gate with a thought and stared, as world after world spun by in a dizzying fashion. Glimpses of raw, empty expanses lit by dozens of red-hot suns flashed past his eyes as he searched for the one world he needed. Any number of hells existed alongside this world. And though the heavenly dimensions were just as many, the gates to those were always sealed.

No one was looking to escape heaven.

But to a demon, these gates were the road to a different sort of paradise. An opening into the world of humans where any number of cruelties could be found and enjoyed. And so the Guardians protected the gates. Beat the demons back as they sneaked through the portals.

Rogan's job was to send those demons back to their hells—not to enter after them. Though it could be done, since a Guardian could survive in the toxic atmospheres of a demon world, he could also be caught there, bound by a demon. Or wounded so desperately it would take centuries to heal.

Yet, there was little choice, and to be honest with himself, Rogan knew he would do this even if there were an alternative. He needed the coming battle to clear his mind of too many other images. Of too many memories and desires.

He needed the fight to stay sane.

"Hold," he said abruptly, his voice quiet but filled with power. The world he sought lay before him, the gate lay open, revealing a darkness beyond the portal. Rogan could see only vaguely flickering lights, like the flames of a thousand candles, dancing in the dark.

Gathering the power within himself, he stepped through the portal and entered a different kind of hell. Instantly, he crouched, gripping his weapons as he swept the area. Not a demon world at all. More of a chamber. Huge and black, with walls of living white flame at either end of the room. And a smaller, narrower doorway in the middle of it all burned with bright orange-and-red flames, casting dancing patterns on the walls and the faces of the people wandering aimlessly through the place.

Rogan slipped into the crowd, unnoticed by the mortals, who cried and wailed and tried to find an escape. They ran and walked and careened into each other and off the walls like billiard balls. And through the crowd, small, scaled demons moved, taunting, biting, screeching until the walls themselves should have bled from the noise and the terror streaking the air.

Rogan kept moving, sliding in and out of the crowd, unnoticed still, both by the mortals and by the demons intent on their prey. He watched as what looked like tiny plums were forced on the humans and when they refused to eat, they were killed, their bodies tossed into the wall of white flames, incinerated in an instant. More screams lifted and the demons howled.

Rogan leaped forward, unable to observe any-more without doing something to help. He swung his broadsword in a wide arc, decapitating the demon closest to him, and as demon blood foun-tained, screams lifted into the air. Human and demon alike ran from him as he dispatched one then another of the creatures.

And while he fought, he saw others eat the fruit. Some died instantly, collapsing in on themselves, while others seemed to go mad before his eyes and joined in with the demons in trying to defeat him. Again and again, he lifted his sword, jabbed the dagger, taking as many of the enemy as he could. The heat in the place was overpowering, the flames bleeding into the room as if trying to reach for him, to devour him.

His mighty arms ached, and his throat was raw with the cinders and the heat. Sweat dripped into his eyes and still he fought, his heart pounding in his chest, his blood pumping ferociously through his veins. He would fight until he could no longer lift his sword. He would kill until there was nothing left standing. Over and over they came at him, and he fought them back. One demon and another. There were always more and his mind emptied but for thoughts of the battle. Thoughts of victory churning inside him.

Behind him, the few mortals who had not tasted the fruit gathered together, as if looking for safety in numbers. They wouldn't be safe, though, Rogan knew. And in that instant, their terror and their cries broke through the veil of red-hazed rage clouding his vision, and he knew his duty lay in more than killing. It was protection that drove him now.

The vicious little demons tore at him as he moved, their teeth and claws ripping at his skin, tearing pieces from his body as though they could nibble him away to nothing if given enough time. The pain in his body was nothing, though. He fought through it, past it, and finally reached those who waited.

With a wave of his hand, he reopened the portal to the human world and shouted, "Go! Go now, all of you!"

He held off the demons as they frantically fought to regain their captives. His sword sang in the blistering air. It dripped with the black, corrosive blood of the demons it had killed and shone in the fiery light with the gleam of death.

Rogan gave one last mighty sweep of that sword, took out three more of the scaly little bastards, then stepped backward through the portal, closing it behind him.

Chest heaving, he drew in the sweet, clean air of the earth he'd chosen so long ago to defend. The night was cold, and while he'd been gone, the wind had lifted again, carrying the scent of the lake, the meadows, the heart that was Ireland, to him. His strong arms trembled, and the blades in his hands hung limp at his sides. The battle was done for the moment, and all that was left was the adrenaline still crashing through his system.

The crying around him slowly shook Rogan out of his battle-induced frenzy. The soft sobs and whimpers brought him back to the world of the living, where the survivors of that demon holding dimension looked at him through shattered eyes. He felt their pain, raw and desperate, sensed their fears, their need for solace. And he knew that he could give them the only gift that mattered at the moment.

He would do this for their sakes…and for his own.

The mortal world wasn't meant to know of demons and Guardians and the other creatures that lived just beyond the reach of reason. And so he linked his mind to theirs, each in turn, and wiped their short-term memories. Their tears dried and their fears melted away as Rogan took their pain for his own, leaving only a confused sense of peace behind.

Where they'd been and what they'd survived would be lost to them forever behind a cloud of fog in their minds. They would wonder where they'd been. How they'd come to be here in the middle of the night.

But they would never recall just what had happened and so, would never remember the one man who'd saved them all—yet couldn't find a way to save himself.

Chapter 11

Rogan!

Aly wasn't surprised when he didn't answer her. He'd blocked her for hours, the mental barriers he erected like steel doors, keeping her from reading his thoughts, knowing what he was feeling, experiencing. Even worse than that, though, she knew he heard her when she called him and was simply ignoring her insistent mental call.

It tore at her, not knowing where he was and what was happening. Not hearing the comforting sound of his roar telling her to leave him alone, and Aly knew, as she paced his library like a caged animal, that she was in for years of just this feeling.

When she and Rogan parted, she'd never know where he was, *how* he was. If he was thinking of her, missing her. If he had loved her as she loved him.

Oh, God, she did love him.

"What a mess," she whispered, and her voice was lost in the crackle of the fire in the hearth. Rubbing her arms with her hands, she stared around the library as if just noticing where she was. The room was dimly lit—only the fire gave off light and heat—because at the moment, Aly was more comfortable in the shadows than in the light.

Her chest ached; her heart twisted with the pain of knowing she'd already lost him. *I won't go down this road with you again, Alison.* The words he'd said to her seemed to echo over and over again in her mind, and every time they did, she heard the finality in them.

He wouldn't risk trusting her with his love again. Wouldn't trust her not to run.

And how could she blame him? He hadn't asked her to be with him now, hadn't offered her his love, but if he had, would she be brave enough to accept it? To accept him? Would she be willing to somehow become an Immortal and eventually lose her sister and her friends and everything she loved to the passage of time?

She didn't know. Couldn't be sure. Just thinking about it made her anxious, and though she hated that knowledge, she couldn't hide from it. Even knowing she loved him, there was a part of her that cringed from the immortality thing. To join Rogan's world, she would have to leave her own world behind. Yes, she would still have her sister for now…if she could find a way to restore Casey to her own mind, but it would be different. They would be different.

"God, I'm still a coward," she muttered and saw no clear way out of the hole she'd dug for herself.

When the front door opened, and Rogan stepped into the foyer, she ran to him. "Rogan, oh, thank God."

He looked at her, his eyes empty, distant; that look stopped her in her tracks. "Don't."

"Don't what? Worry? Too late," she snapped and went toward him anyway, silently challenging him to try to stop her. He only sighed, and his huge body seemed to sag as if he were too tired to hold himself upright.

His shirt and pants were torn and bloodstained. His eyes were shadowed, and his features were tight with pain he wouldn't acknowledge.

"You're hurt."

"It's nothing."

"All of that blood came from somewhere, Rogan."

"Not all of it's mine." Wincing, he pulled off his long, black coat, tossed it across the newel post and started up the stairs. "I'm for a shower and bed. We'll talk of this in the morning."

"You're wounded."

"'Tis nothing."

"*'Tis* bleeding."

He glanced back at her. "Not any longer. They'll heal. Now leave me be, Alison."

She was right behind him. She'd been waiting for what felt like hours, every second ticking away more slowly than the last. Maggie had long since gone to bed and Casey was insensible, so Aly had waited, alone, terrified.

His steps were heavy and quick, but she kept pace as she started up the stairs after him. Tired as he was, his mental barriers slipped a bit and gave her a brief glimpse of what he'd been through. She fisted one hand to her chest and bit down hard on her bottom lip as she raced through his thoughts before he could shut her out again.

The firelit darkness. The demons, tearing at him with teeth and claws. The people, dying, screaming. Walls of flame and bodies tossed into them like kindling.

"God, Rogan…"

He stopped on the stairs, gripped the banister tight enough to make his knuckles white and said softly, "You shouldn't have looked."

"You're right. I shouldn't have had to look. You should have told me."

"It's not for you to bear," he insisted. "This has nothing to do with you."

She grabbed at his arm and felt the muscles beneath her hand bunch. "Nothing to do with me? It's only because of my sister you went there at all."

Rogan looked down at her hand on his arm, and she could have sworn she felt heat slant into her body from the power in that gaze alone. Finally, though, he looked into her eyes. "What I do I do because I choose it. Because I made a vow. Now go, will you?"

What was unsaid rang in her heart. He made a vow and he kept it. When she—or Sinead—had made a vow to love him, she'd thrown it aside and ran like a frightened child. His word was all. Hers had meant nothing.

"I'm not *her.*" Aly said the words aloud as much for herself as for him. Then, instead of leaving him, she stepped up onto the stair beside him, lifted his right arm and laid it over her shoulders. "I'll help, then I'll leave."

He looked down at her for a long moment or two. "You've a hard head, Alison Blair."

"And it takes one to know one, Rogan Butler."

Shaking his head, he started up the stairs again, and Aly moved with him, feeling him holding himself back from her even as she tried to help. She supposed it was never easy for a strong man to need help. And for him to require it of her must have been even more difficult.

But the feel of his body along hers, the weight of his arm on her shoulders, the brush of his hair against her cheek—all of it felt so right. And she knew that without him she'd never be whole again, never be totally complete. She'd be like a puzzle with the center piece lost. The picture she made would always be unfinished.

"I'm fine now. Go on." He straightened up at the head of the stairs and gave her a look that she supposed he thought was terrifying.

"You might as well give it up. I'm here and I'm going to help whether you like it or not." They walked into his bedroom, and Aly closed the door behind them. "Take off your shirt so I can see how bad it is."

He didn't, though. "Do you think this is the first time I've taken some hits from some bloody demons? It's not and I've done well for myself up till now. I don't need you, Alison."

Well, that cut to the heart of her. "You have me anyway. Now take off the shirt."

Muttering a streak of Gaelic, he did it, tearing the buttons free to send them snapping around the room like tiny missiles. Then he shrugged out of his shirt and dropped it onto the floor. Spreading his arms wide, he said, "Have your look, then, and be off."

Tears filled her eyes. Teeth marks. Knife slashes. Burns. Dozens of painful marks stippled his broad, sculpted chest. She reached out to lay her fingers on one of the gashes on his pecs, and he flinched from her as though she brought him more pain than the fresh wounds. Aly pulled her hand back, curling her fingers into her palm, bit down on her bottom lip and walked a slow circle around him. He was covered in bruises, wounds, burns.

And though the wounds themselves looked raw and painful, they'd already stopped bleeding. The gift of immortality, she guessed. Still, the wash of dried blood stained his flesh in shades of rust and black.

"Seen enough?" he demanded.

"Is the rest of you this torn up, too?" she asked, coming around to stand in front of him again.

He scowled. "Just a few burns on me legs. They'll be fine."

"Yeah, I know. You told me." She looked around the room and asked, "Where's that magic salve of yours?"

"I'll take care of it." He turned his back on her and headed for the bathroom.

"I'll help."

He stopped dead. "Do you not understand I don't want you here?"

"That was plain enough," she said, despite the knot in her throat. "So, yes, I get it. But I'm not leaving until you're taken care of."

He spun around to glare at her. "Having you here, wanting you, tears at me. Is it your plan, then, to bring me to my knees, woman?"

"Of course not." Shocked, she stared at him and tried to tell him with her eyes that she cared for him. She knew he wouldn't want to hear the words, but she hoped he would look into her mind, her heart.

When she didn't feel his mental touch, though, she gave up on that hope and spoke instead. "What you're doing for me, for Casey, that means something to me. It means *everything* to me. And I want to help you."

He sighed, leaning his head back as if looking to heaven for answers, and then asked, "Will it get rid of you that much sooner?"

"Yes," she said, hating that he wanted her gone. Hating that she didn't have the right to make him listen to her. Hating that she wanted to touch him so badly that her hands itched with it.

"Fine, then. Do it and be done."

He walked into the bathroom ahead of her, and Aly had only a moment or two to look around the opulent room. What looked like miles of gleaming white-and-green tile shone in the brilliant light that streamed down from overhead fixtures. A mirror as long as the room itself took up one wall, and directly opposite it was a shower built for six.

Roughened green tile swept up the entire wall, and four shining silver showerheads at varying heights and angles jutted out from the wall. There was no back to the shower, so anyone in there would be exposed to the room. To the mirror, she thought, sweeping a glance at her own reflection staring back at her.

Her heart pounded, and her body flickered to rampant life, her core becoming a heated slick of welcome for a man who would no doubt refuse to touch her. And, God, she wanted him to touch her again. Wanted him inside her again. Even if it were the last time...no, especially if it were to be the last time, she wanted to feel his hard, thick, huge body filling hers, erupting into hers. She wanted to hold his broad shoulders and feel his tremors as a climax took him, and she wanted to ride him to a release that would be hard enough to paralyze her.

"Alison?"

Her gaze slipped to meet his in the mirror. He was watching her. And, she realized a heartbeat later, he was *reading* her. Seeing her thoughts, hearing her desires, experiencing the heat that now threatened to swamp her.

"Rogan, I..."

"You shouldn't have come to me tonight." His features were cold and hard, but his eyes lit with a green fire that blazed a path straight down to her soul.

"I had to see you. Had to—"

"You should go," he said, his lips hardly moving, his voice no more than a choked-off guttural groan. "Go now, before there is no leaving. For either of us."

"I don't want to," she whispered, still watching his reflection, still lost in the fire of his eyes.

"Thank God." He grabbed her from behind, and in the mirror she watched his strong, muscular arms come around her. She kept her gaze fixed on the shining glass reflecting the two of them together as his hands tore the buttons from her shirt. He yanked the blouse from her body, and she felt the cool air of the room press against her skin.

She wasn't cold, though. Couldn't be cold ever again—not with the way his eyes looked at her. He tore the clasp of her bra, as if he couldn't bear the thought of anything between his hands and the feel of her. And when that bit of lace was gone, his big palms cupped her breasts. His thumbs and fore-fingers tweaked and pulled at her nipples, and she watched.

Watched her reflection push her breasts harder into his touch. She watched his hands slide up and down her body. Watched as his fingers nimbly undid the snap and zipper of her jeans. Watched breathlessly as those magical, strong hands of his slid down beneath the elastic of her panties and touched the heated heart of her.

"Rogan!" At the first touch of his fingers, her body splintered, as if it had been waiting only for that. Only for the barest brush of his skin on hers to send her into waves and waves of rippling ecstasy.

With one hand on her breast, he used the other

to take her. To touch and stroke. To delve into her heat and caress her from the inside. Her eyes closed on the sensations pouring through her. She couldn't bear it. Couldn't survive it all.

"Open your eyes." The order came fast and hard and so close to her ear that she felt the brush of his breath on her skin. "Open your eyes and see yourself as I see you. See yourself come for me."

His body pressed into hers and she felt his erection, thick and hard, through his leather pants, as it pushed against her bottom. She moved her hips, rubbing, stroking, welcoming, and then she opened her eyes as he'd ordered and caught a glimpse of her own eyes, wild and needy.

The image they made together set her blood on fire. His huge body wrapped around hers. His hands touching her so intimately. His fingers pushing up higher and higher inside her. She tried to open her legs for him, wanting more, needing more. But her damned jeans were in the way.

He read that thought, chuckled low in his throat and in the blink of an eye had her naked in front of the mirror. His hands moved all over her skin, his battle-scarred flesh caressing her smooth body. There was no curve, no crevice he didn't explore. And it wasn't enough.

"I need you," she whispered, aching for him, writhing for him, her body a quivering mass of electrified nerve endings. "I need you inside me."

Sweeping one thick arm around her middle, he turned her around and planted her feet in the shower stall. Then he peeled off his leathers, joined her and turned on the water. Instantly, hot jets of water streamed from the four nozzles. She was hit from all sides, by the fast and furious pulses. Her body felt alive in a way it never had been before, and when he pulled her to him, Aly knew this was home.

This man.

These arms.

This place.

He whispered words in Gaelic that sounded so beautiful to her she wanted to weep for it. His mouth trailed down from her forehead, across her eyes, to her cheeks and then her mouth. His tongue swept across her lips as if he were tasting her, and her heart quivered.

Then he dipped lower still and followed the line of her throat with his teeth and tongue. Shivers of expectation rolled through her, and Aly held on to his slick, wet shoulders just to keep herself grounded. When he bent and took first one nipple and then the other into his mouth, rolling his tongue across the sensitive tip, she whimpered and arched into him, silently pleading for more.

You're more beautiful every time I touch you.

His voice whispered through her mind, and she felt as well as heard his words.

My body aches for yours, he said as he suckled her breast, drawing, tugging, pulling at her flesh until she cried his name on a broken sigh. She felt his erection, hard and thick, pressing into her and wiggled against him eagerly.

Straightening up, he palmed some clear green liquid from a soap dispenser built into the wall, and then he smoothed the fresh scent of it over her skin, over his own. He turned her in his arms, and while Aly rubbed the soap over his broad, battered body, he did the same for her. His fingers swept along her spine, down to her bottom. The soapy, slick feel of him tingled over her skin and made her feel both soothed and excited. Then he held her to the jets pulsing from the wall until the soap was sliding free of their bodies to swirl at their feet.

I must have you now. I must be inside you, hard and deep.

Yes, Rogan, she said, looking over her shoulder into his eyes. *Hard and deep.*

With a groan, he bent her over until she could lean against the end wall and planted both hands firmly on the roughened tile. He stood behind her in the steamy room, and with one hand he parted her legs with an intimate caress. She moved back into him, offering herself to him, riding the near-electric charge shooting through her.

Once, twice, he stroked her deepest folds, feeling the slickness of her, parting her, readying her. Her hips rocked back against him. She sighed, on the edge of a precipice, waiting impatiently for what she knew was coming.

When he pushed himself inside her, Aly groaned and felt him slide so deep inside her she was sure he'd touched her heart. She pushed back against him, twisting, moving with him, finding the rhythm he set. Again and again he moved within her, long, sure strokes that drove them both toward a peak that climbed ever higher. He reached beneath her and cupped one of her breasts as if he couldn't touch her enough, and with that tender stroking caress, Aly felt the first of the tremors clatter through her body.

Take all of me, he whispered into her mind.

Deliberately, Aly turned her head so that she could see them in the mirror. And watching her huge Guardian lay claim to her body and soul was the final push she needed to tumble over the edge of reason and into the whirlpool of sensation.

Mentally, she reached for him and sent him all she was feeling on a purr of incredible satisfaction. And a moment later she felt his own release and heard both him within her mind and the guttural groan he roared into the room.

An hour later they were in his massive bed. Aly lay stretched along the length of his body, and she was no more than a supple puddle of goo. She couldn't have moved if it had meant her life.

Beneath her Rogan stirred, stroking one hand down the length of her, fingertips gliding across her skin. "Thanks for your help," he said, and she heard the smile in his voice.

Lifting her head with great effort, she looked down at him and caught the barest glimmer of that smile still remaining on his lips. "Believe me when I say, my pleasure."

He tucked her hair back behind her ear, stroked her cheek and said, "But you know, this night changes nothing."

She stiffened a bit and felt a tiny kernel of cold settle in her belly. "Rogan..."

"Hush now," he told her and shook his head on the pillow. "What we shared tonight is in the way of a goodbye, I'm thinking. Once we've dealt with the demon, you'll take your sister and go."

"I don't want to leave you again."

"Ah, Alison, it's best if you do and you know it." He framed her face with his big hands and drew her down for one sweet, brief kiss. "I want you to know I'm glad we had this night. I'm glad we found each other again, if only for a short time. I mourned you so in that long-ago time, and I'm pleased to know your soul lives on. But there's no middle ground between us. I'm still an Immortal."

Her heart sank at the words because she knew he was right. His immortality wasn't something they could get past or ignore. "You could become human," she said quietly. "Guardians have done it before, given up immortality for a normal life."

Now he did smile. "And what would I do with this normal life?" he asked her ruefully. "I'm an ancient Celtic warrior. Is there much call for that sort of thing in these times?"

She bit her lip and stared into green eyes she knew would haunt her for the rest of time.

"No," he said, reading her regret, her sorrow. "I'm born to fight. It's all I know. And I made a vow long ago."

"Michael, there's no other choice." Rogan looked at the being across the room from him and had the urge to shield his eyes from the brilliant white light that always seemed to surround the man. "To kill Balam, I must go into his dimension. And maybe then the mortals he's changed will return to themselves."

"There's no guarantee of that," Michael said, walking around the library, peeking into drawers, looking at the books on the shelves. "It's a dangerous thing for any Guardian to be in a demon world, and you know it."

This kind of talk was exactly why Rogan had refused to allow Alison to be in the room during his meeting with Michael. He didn't want her worried, and more than that he didn't want to dash her hopes if Michael told him there was no hope for Casey. He hadn't, yet. But the possibility was still there.

To be certain she didn't pick up on any of his thoughts, though, Rogan kept his mental blocks firmly in place. And as for anything Michael might say—well, he was too powerful a being to be overheard if he didn't wish to be.

"I do," Rogan said. "But I've gone in before."

"And barely made it out with your skin intact," Michael reminded him with a pointed look.

Rogan huffed out an impatient breath. "There's no other way for it. Alison's sister is demented. And the others I freed last night are only the tip of this demon's iceberg."

"Demons with delusions of grandeur," Michael muttered, opening up the bookshelves to reveal the bar. Helping himself to a straight, short shot of whiskey, he looked into the glass before swallowing the liquor down and asked, "Can there be anything more dangerous?"

"Not to my mind," Rogan said.

"You're an Immortal," Michael said softly, "but you can be grievously wounded."

"That I bloody well know."

"*Or,*" Michael continued as if Rogan hadn't spoken, "you could be captured, held prisoner for eternity, suffering tortures unimaginable."

Though that didn't sound like something he'd care for, Rogan brushed the worry of it aside. He wouldn't be captured. There was no demon alive strong enough or quick enough to manage that.

Setting his glass down, Michael asked, "And what of Alison Blair?"

"What of her?" Rogan's voice was stiffer, harsher, and though he realized it, he couldn't stop it. He didn't want to talk about Alison with Michael. Hell, the man had known for centuries that Sinead/Alison was born again, but had he ever mentioned it? Indeed he had not.

"Are you going to let her walk out of your life again?"

"Surely that's my own business."

Michael shrugged and walked across the room to stare out the windows at the silver surface of the Lough. "It is. I only wondered."

"Wondered be damned," Rogan barked. "You could have told me," he accused, stabbing the air with his index finger. "You could have let me know that Sinead had been reborn."

"So you could spend eternity looking for her?"

Grumbling, Rogan pushed his hair back from his face and glared at the man he'd called friend for centuries. "Worried I wouldn't fight your demons for you?"

"No," Michael said with a smile. "You're a man of your word, Rogan Butler. Always have been." He dropped into a chair, crossed one foot over a knee and tapped his fingers against the arm of the chair. "But you would have looked for her."

"And why shouldn't I?"

"Because that's not how it's done," Michael said. "A Guardian finds his or her Mate when the time is right. Not before."

"Oh, aye." Rogan snorted and headed for the liquor cabinet himself now, early afternoon be damned. "As when I found Sinead the first time. Oh, yes, Michael. That time was certainly right." He poured a drink, tossed it back and sneered at the other man. "She was afraid of me. My life."

Michael nodded. "True. Sinead wasn't ready, but the Fates must have thought she might be."

"Bugger the Fates and bugger you, for that matter," Rogan snapped. "I'll not be a dog on a leash for any of you. Come here, go there, stay, Rogan. No. I'll fight demons for it's what I'm good at. But as to the other, I'll thank you to keep out of it."

Michael's features went hard and cool as he pushed up from the chair. "Do what you like about your Mate. It's your business, as you say. As to the other, I'll remind you that the only way for a human to leave a demon dimension is through sacrifice."

"That's bloody vague, isn't it?" Rogan scrubbed both hands over his face, feeling his antagonism fade as he did so. "I know about the sacrifice. I'm prepared for that."

"Are you?"

"I am," Rogan said, then looked his old friend in the eye. "I've a favor to ask though."

"Anything."

"If I don't make it out, watch over Alison for me. See that she's taken care of."

Michael nodded solemnly and offered his hand. "My word on it."

Chapter 12

Rogan spent the next full day preparing for his coming foray into the demon dimension.

"You'll wait here, with Casey." The ring of command was in Rogan's voice, and it was all Aly could do not to smack him.

Ever since leaving that meeting with Michael, Rogan had been gathering weapons, readying himself for the trip back into the demon dimension. Along with preparing physically, he was pulling back from her emotionally, as well. He was, once again, the cold, aloof Guardian she'd met the first night she'd come to his house.

"Are you listening?"

"Hard not to listen to a voice that rattles window-panes," she muttered.

He sighed in response. One of those completely male, I'm-trying-to-be-patient sighs that irritated women faster than anything else. "I know you're worried."

"Damn right I'm worried. And not just about Casey, either. Rogan, there's no guarantee you'll come back out of there."

He actually looked insulted. "This is not the first time I've done battle in a demon world. I've yet to be defeated."

Good, she wanted to say. Thank God, she thought about adding. Instead, she sat silently as he packed his long, black coat with weapons. Knives, wicked daggers with curved blades, throwing stars. The Guardian netting was tucked into an inside pocket, and then he went to work on a shoulder holster he'd pulled from his closet. No guns, just scabbards for yet more knives. He was a walking arsenal, yet she couldn't help wishing he was armed with, oh, say, a rocket launcher. Or at the very least, a machine gun.

But she knew the fighting rules of the Guardians as well as he did. No guns were ever used, because the fear was that a civilian could be killed far more easily by a stray bullet. When a Guardian fought, he did it hand to hand, up close and personal.

"How are you going to do it? I mean, what's the

plan?" she asked, when she couldn't bear the silence another moment.

He glanced at her before saying, "It would be easier on you to not know."

"You're wrong." Nothing was going to make this easy on her. She wouldn't breathe a calm breath until he was back from the demon world and Casey was herself again. "I'll feel better if I know what you're planning. Knowing is always better than *not* knowing, Rogan."

Looking at her for a long moment, he acknowledged, "I can see where that might be truth." He blew out a breath and walked toward her. Stopping directly in front of her, he said, "I'll go to that holding room again. Free whatever humans I can and then go into the dimension itself."

He said it as calmly as another man might say, *Well, I'll be stopping at a pub. Then I'll pick up the milk at the market.* There was no fear in him. She looked at him and only read his strength. His self-confidence, not arrogance. Just a belief in himself that few men had. He had been doing this very thing for nearly a thousand years. He'd fought demons in this world and in others. He'd always survived. He'd always won.

She tried to cling to that knowledge, but a small voice in the back of her mind whispered that *everyone* lost at some point. No one could win all the time.

Shaking that thought free of her mind, she looked up at him. "Then what? You go into Balam's dimension and…"

"And I kill him."

"That's it? That's the plan?" She pushed off the edge of the bed, took a few angry, hurried strides, then whipped back around to look at him. "What if you can't find him? What if he has a demon army waiting for you? What if—"

"This does no good," Rogan said. His features were cold and stiff, his green eyes shadowed with a resolve she knew she would never be able to shatter. And would she if she could? He was a warrior. Big. Proud. Strong. This was who he was. His purpose in life. He'd dedicated his eternity to protecting those who desperately needed it.

She couldn't, not even in her fear for him, ask him to be less than he was.

"You'll wait here," he said, which was more of a statement than a question.

"I don't have much choice, do I?"

"You don't, no." He gave her a half smile to take the sting out of it, but added, "It's better this way, Alison."

No, it wasn't. She wanted to be with him, to face whatever was happening at his side. But she didn't stand a chance of changing his mind. "Will I be able to stay linked with you, at least?"

"No." He walked across the room and grabbed

a long strip of leather; gathering his hair at the nape of his neck, he tied the mass off so that it hung down to the middle of his back in a single tail. Looking at her in the mirror, he said, "Maintaining the link between us will distract me and upset you."

"Oh, sure. Don't want to upset the little woman."

"Seems to me you're already upset," he pointed out. Then he turned around, walked past her to the bed and picked up his shoulder harness. Slipping it on, he snapped it together in the middle of his chest, then checked the knives to make sure they pulled free of the leather scabbards easily.

When he picked up his coat and pulled it on, he looked at her again and said, "This is for me to do, Alison. You'll have to trust that I'll get it done. That all will be well."

"That's a lot of trust."

"Aye, it is." He met her gaze, staring into her eyes with an intensity that seemed to steal her breath. She felt his strength even at a distance, and it was all she could do to keep from throwing herself at him.

Nothing between them was resolved—and now he was leaving. Going off to a battle with a demon whose only objective would be to tear Rogan apart.

Five hundred years ago, the woman she had been hadn't trusted Rogan enough. She'd let her fears cloud her mind and turn her heart. She'd run from the love he'd offered her and the life they might have made together.

Because she hadn't trusted Rogan.

Or herself.

Aly wouldn't make that same mistake. What was the point of reincarnation if you didn't learn from your past lives?

"Fine," she said, feeling the physical sensation of cold when he closed his mind to her. The absence of his touch was palpable and left her feeling bereft. But if he could close her out, then it would work the other way, too. If he wasn't maintaining their link, then he wouldn't know what Aly was doing, would he?

"Good luck," she said quietly, and he walked up to her, reaching for her chin, cupping it in his palm.

"Don't be afraid, Alison. I'll see you soon."

She grabbed his hand and held on. "You'd better."

He smiled, grabbed his sword, then walked out of the bedroom. Pausing in the open doorway, he looked back and inclined his head in a courtly, old-world gesture that made her heart turn over in her chest.

Then he was gone.

Rogan walked to the portal. Evening stretched out across the countryside, dappling the world in lengthening shadows. He became a part of the coming night. He felt the land beneath his feet. The cold slap of the Irish wind. He scented the Lough and the hint of chimney smoke in the air.

He wanted to ground himself in this world before entering that very different one. He hadn't lied to Alison. Maintaining the link between them while he tried to fight would only splinter a concentration he was going to need.

But at the same time, he could admit, if only to himself, that he missed the feel of her in his mind. Missed that connection that allowed him to hear the quick clip of her thoughts.

She was so much more than she'd once been. She was braver, stronger. And more stubborn as well. Alison wasn't afraid to stand toe-to-toe with him and fight for what she believed, wanted. He let himself remember the past few days in vivid detail. Every expression on her face. Every thought in her mind. He knew her better than mortal men would know a woman after twenty years together.

And he loved her. Even more than he once had loved Sinead.

With that thought clear in his mind, Rogan stopped at the edge of the lake and turned back for another look at his house. Lights flared from the windows. A twist of smoke lifted from each of the chimneys. The night sky behind the house seemed brilliant with stars.

"Be safe," he said quietly. "No matter the outcome tonight, be safe."

He pulled in a deep breath, then deliberately turned his back on the house where Alison waited.

Rogan realized that for the first time in his too long life, he was leaving something behind him as he went off to fight. And he prayed that perhaps in another life, they would have the chance at love that had eluded them throughout time.

Slowly, resolutely, he walked toward the ruined keep and the portal.

Aly didn't have much time.

Maggie was downstairs; the clatter of dishes being loaded into the dishwasher was clear enough to carry through the house. But the woman was a working fiend. There was no telling how quickly she'd be finished and come looking for Alison.

Hurrying, Aly ran to her room and dragged a heavy, dark green sweater over her head. Her jeans would have to do, but she changed out of her sneakers and into a pair of boots. Rushing into the adjoining bathroom, she couldn't even look herself in the eye as she rummaged through her things for an elastic band. Once she had it, she pulled her hair into a ponytail, then raced out toward Rogan's room.

She'd spent enough time in there to know where he kept most of his weapons. Heading directly into a closet the size of her bedroom at home, she ran to the back, to a set of built-in cabinets. They weren't locked—who would try to steal anything from a man like Rogan? She opened the cabinet doors and stared at the treasure trove of carnage. Daggers, swords, knives, clubs...the man could outfit his own private war.

"Well, he does fight his own little wars every night, doesn't he?" she whispered and helped herself to a lethal-looking dagger.

The handle was leather-wrapped steel, and the blade glinted like a new coin in the light. She rummaged around until she found a scabbard for the thing, then she slid it through the belt loop on her jeans and tugged the hem of her sweater down over it.

She might be risking a few things tonight, but she wasn't stupid. She'd go into the demon world armed, at least. Rogan wasn't going to be happy to see her, but that couldn't be helped. And who knew? Maybe he'd be glad for her help.

Weapon taken care of, she sprinted down the hall to where Casey was being kept.

Her heart thudded painfully in her chest, and breath seemed hard to come by. Her mind was a whirl of thoughts that she had to keep reminding herself to keep blocked from Rogan.

She'd been planning this since overhearing Rogan and Michael's council of war. Yes, killing the demon was important, but her sister was important, too. Rogan was so determined to keep her and Casey out of danger that he hadn't considered the fact that just maybe, Casey *had* to be there when the demon was killed.

What if proximity counted in ending the compulsion, or whatever it was the demon had done to Casey? If Aly kept her sister here, then she might be trapped like this for the rest of her life. A prisoner of her own body. Locked away in an institution somewhere.

"No *way.*" Aly ground her teeth together, took the key off the hook in the wall and shoved it into the door. Turning it, she opened the door and walked inside. The empty room looked as grim as before. The light was dim but bright enough to showcase Casey, still bound on the floor. Still rolling about as if she couldn't bear to remain unmoving, driven by the evil invading her body. Still chanting and singing and talking to herself.

Still on the wrong side of sanity.

"Casey?"

She stopped, tossed her dirty blond hair out of her face and stared. Her eyes were black, and when they fixed on Aly in a cold glare, Aly fought the overwhelming urge to run.

This was her little sister, and she would *not* let her end up like this. No matter what she had to do…or, thinking of Rogan now, who she had to stand up to, she was going to find a way to bring Casey back.

Aly walked into the room with quiet, careful steps. Easing up next to her sister, she went down on one knee and looked into those eyes that were so unfamiliar, so empty, they made her want to shiver. "Casey, it's me. Aly."

Her sister smiled, and the action was chilling. "I know you…"

Aly's stomach curdled. "You said Balam wants me dead, right?"

"My master," she crooned, as if summoning a lover. "Dead, dead, all dead."

Aly swallowed hard and curled her fingers into fists so tight that her nails dug into her palms. She had to breathe through her nose because her stomach was churning with such an intense nausea that it was all she could do to keep from retching. "What if you don't kill me?" she asked, keeping her voice a low hush. "What if you take me to him instead?"

Casey's gaze narrowed. "My master would be pleased."

"Excellent," Aly said, really wanting to meet this damn demon herself anyway. She'd never considered herself a violent kind of person. She'd always been the quiet type. The research drone. Happiest when surrounded by the musty smell of books. But tonight, staring down into her sister's eyes and seeing only a stranger, she could cheerfully slam her stolen dagger into Balam's chest herself. "So you'll take me to him?"

"Yes. Yes, he will be very pleased with me."

"Well, that's all that counts, right?" Aly kept her

voice quiet, though her eyes were wary and every nerve in her body felt tensed, poised for fight or flight. "So, I'll untie you and you'll take me to Balam, right?"

Casey's eyes gleamed like black marble. There was no light in their depths. No life, only a soul-shuddering darkness that seemed as deep and old as time. "I will take you to him, and he will kill you himself. A great honor."

"Right." Aly bent to Casey's feet and tore at the thickly knotted ropes binding her. When she had a little trouble, she slipped her dagger free and the razor-sharp blade sliced through the bonds with a whisper of sound. The ropes fell free and Casey stretched aching, cramped muscles.

Pushing herself to a sitting position, Casey twisted half around and behind her back, held out her bound wrists.

"No," Aly told her and watched those black eyes shimmer with hatred. "No, your hands stay tied, honey."

And her dagger, Aly thought, curling her fingers around the thick hilt, stayed out. Not that she would ever use it on Casey. Wouldn't be able to. But maybe whatever was inside her little sister would be threatened enough by the dagger's presence to keep things on an even keel until they got to the demon world.

Dragging Casey to her feet, Aly gave her a smile and said, "You ready? Then let's go."

* * *

In the heat of the fire-lit demon holding room, Rogan fought with the strength and determination of ten Guardians. The demons guarding the humans had reacted quickly to his presence once the initial surprise had worn off.

As Rogan moved in and out of the crowd, he kept one eye on the mortals clustering against the back wall and the other on his opponents. Apparently his attack before had warned Balam, because there were at least a dozen more demons here than there had been on Rogan's last visit.

The demons rushed him from different directions, howls tearing through the hot, still air. Their claws and teeth tore at him, but he was single-minded in his fight. He hardly felt the slashes in his flesh, the distinct burn of demon venom as it coursed hungrily through his veins. He had only one objective in mind, and there was room for nothing else.

Free the captives and defeat Balam.

Again and again, he swung his sword, the blade singing as it whistled through the air. Over and over again, he cut down one nasty little fiend only to find another had leaped up to take its place.

Demon blood ran thick in the room, and the stench rose as the unbearable heat fermented the black liquid spreading across the floor. The captured mortals sobbed. Some of the men tried to fight, as if recognizing that they'd been given this one chance to either defend themselves or die with honor. Those humans who were already lost walked through the wall of living flame into what Rogan knew had to be Balam's dimension.

He leaped over a cluster of demons, landing on the balls of his feet and spinning around with such grace that his opponents were momentarily startled. He used those few seconds to reach into his pocket for the Guardian netting. He swung it high with one hand, and it settled back to earth, trapping three of the little monsters within its folds. Then he reached into yet another pocket while swinging his sword in a wide arc, grabbed a throwing star and sent it spinning, point over point, into the chest of another demon preparing to attack.

The rage- and pain-filled scream echoed out around him.

And while Rogan held off the remaining few demons with the tip of his sword, he swung back, to open the portal. Free the mortals, then proceed. But as he moved, that portal lifted, the dark coolness of the human world spilling into this tiny corner of hell.

The trapped mortals raced for freedom. Rogan didn't understand how the damn thing had opened on its own, but he had no time to question it. He could only be grateful that at least some of the mortals were now safe.

Rogan, behind you!

He didn't question how Alison's voice came to him, how she knew what was happening. Rogan only spun into a crouch, swinging one leg out. He knocked the legs out from beneath the attacking demon, and when it was down, he impaled it with his sword. Only then did he realize what had happened.

He turned and looked into Alison's wide eyes.

Get out! He roared the command into her mind even as she fisted a dagger and swiped it at a demon. Casey was beside her and trying to join in the fight. Trying to take her own sister out so the demons could get to her more easily.

"No time to argue," Alison shouted and gave Casey a shove that sent her sprawling. Once her sister was down, Alison ran to him. Her eyes glittered in the hellish light. Her cheeks were flushed, and already sweat beaded on her forehead and upper lip. "I had to be here, Rogan. *Casey* had to be here."

He yanked her to him in a burst of rage-fueled protectiveness and held her tightly to his side as he plunged his sword into the chest of the nearest demon. There were only a few more. He could keep her safe. *Would* keep her safe, no matter what. "Stay beside me."

"I can fight and I will," she said, moving out from under his arm. "You can't hold on to me and move freely. Back-to-back, Rogan. Together. We do this together."

Damn woman. His thoughts were black, furious, but he couldn't stop her. Couldn't send her back. Couldn't argue. He could only race to end this fight as quickly as possible.

He turned, and back-to-back they fought off the last remaining demons. Absentmindedly, he was aware of her skill. Clumsy at first, her movements became more fluid, more thorough. Her strength was no match for his, but her resolve was giving her the power she needed. He heard her shouts, her screams, and read her thoughts, a churning mass of fear and courage. And he knew he loved her as he had never loved another living thing in this life. She was all. She was everything.

They moved together as though they'd been born to be two halves of a whole. As if sensing each other's movements, they turned and dipped and swayed, back-to-back, arms flailing, blades flashing, until at last there was silence. Only the roar of the flames, Casey's frustrated whimpers and their own heavy breathing disrupted the stillness.

And finally, Rogan tossed his sword down to clatter against the bloody floor, grabbed Aly's shoulders and yanked her up to him. Holding her pressed to his length, Rogan breathed in her scent, listened to the frantic pounding of her heart and fought the urge to throttle her.

"Have you taken leave of all your senses, Alison?" He set her back from him, looked down into her eyes and read the stubborn determination shining there. "To come here? To fight? What were you thinking?"

She reached up with one hand and cupped his cheek. Breath still puffing in and out of her lungs, she shook her head and said, "I had to come, Rogan. You didn't want me to, I know. But I had to."

"You have to get out now. While you can. Wait outside the portal for me." He framed her face with his hands. "I will do what needs doing. Trust me."

She reached up and covered his hands with hers. "I do trust you, Rogan." Her gaze speared into his as she struggled to breathe the hot, noxious air. "I'm not the woman I was five hundred years ago. I *love* you."

He reeled with the impact of those three words, whispered so urgently, so fervently. And before he could react to them, she spoke again.

"I know what you are. Who you are. And I love you, Rogan. I'll even stay with you if I can. But you have to trust me, too."

"It's not a question of that."

"It is. At the bottom of it, trust is there. Do you trust me to do what I have to do? To be strong and stand at your side?"

He dropped his hands, bent down and picked up his sword and said, "I don't want you at my side."

He pointed the blade at the wall of ever-shifting, white-hot flames. "Not in there. Not where the very air can kill you with a breath."

"I can go in if I eat the fruit. You know that."

"Bugger that." His hand fisted on the hilt of his sword. "Do you know how many of these mortals I saw keel over with one taste? Dead, Alison. In an instant their bodies tossed into the fire."

She shivered a little despite the heat and took a long, hard breath. "But some of them survived."

"Bloody hell, do you even hear what you're saying to me? *Some* survived? You're willing to chance your life on that fine thread of hope?"

"I don't want to, no. But Casey survived it," she reminded him. "And I'm her sister. That makes the odds more in my favor, right?"

He shook his head, unwilling to listen. But she kept talking anyway, refusing to be shut out.

"Rogan, what if Casey has to actually be present when you kill Balam? If she's not there, she might never be whole again."

He hated that she might be right. He had no idea how the upper-level demon's compulsion was set. If Casey were to have a chance, he would have to take her into the dimension with him and try to keep her safe while facing down the master demon—and however many minions the damn thing controlled.

Alison read him easily. "You can't do both,

Rogan. Don't you see? You can't fight Balam and protect Casey. You need me. I have to be there. I can protect my sister and watch your back while you fight."

He shook his head and wondered how she could look so beautiful, even in the light of demon fire. Wondered how he could possibly even be considering such madness. He couldn't risk her. Even if they were never together, he would know that she was alive and well and living her life. To try to live an eternity with the knowledge that the woman he loved had been lost to demons, not once but *twice,* was more than could be asked of any man—immortal or no.

"Impossible. No human can withstand the atmosphere in a demon dimension for long."

"I can if I eat that fruit."

"And if the fruit doesn't kill you."

"I'm willing to take the risk."

Five hundred years ago she hadn't been able or willing to risk danger for the sake of love. She had changed. Grown. Become stronger.

And he loved her for it. Yet, "I won't risk you."

"You don't get to make that choice." Lifting her chin in defiance, she pointed at her sister and said, "Casey is my family. I can't leave her like that. I can't stand by and do nothing to help her. I *won't.*"

Watching her, loving her, Rogan knew he, too, would have to risk all for her. He had to risk his own fear of losing her. He couldn't keep her from doing what she had to do under the guise of protection. If he did, neither of them would be able to get past it.

He sucked in a great gulp of air, looked around on the battle-strewn ground and spotted a piece of the demon fruit. Picking it up, he wiped it clean on his coat and studied it for a long moment. "Before you eat this," he said, his gaze capturing hers, "I want you to know that I love you."

Her eyes glistened, and in this nightmarish place filled with the stench of death, he had never loved her more, or been more proud.

"You're a woman to stand beside a man, Alison Blair. Your strength humbles me and your courage terrifies me. But I love you as I have loved no other."

"I love you, too, Rogan. I always will."

Lifting her chin, squaring her shoulders, Alison reached for the tiny plum. Her fingers closed over it as she raised it to her mouth.

Then she closed her eyes and took a bite.

Chapter 13

The fruit was bitter, its juice stinging Aly's tongue and the insides of her cheeks as if it were acid. She scrunched up her eyes, shuddered viciously and forced herself to swallow. Instantly, she felt something shift deep within her, as if her organs were easing out of the way to avoid coming into contact with the alien juice.

Alison swayed unsteadily as tendrils of something dark and wicked spiraled through her bloodstream, like black ribbon loosened from a spool.

"You're alive."

"Yeah." She looked up at Rogan, rubbing her forehead as her vision blurred, corrected, then blurred again. "But something's happening to me." She pulled in a breath and then another, hoping to regain her sense of balance. Seeing his worried stare, she said, "We'd better hurry."

Rogan nodded, stalked to where Casey lay trying to right herself and plucked her from the floor as if she were no bigger than a child. She shrieked in his grasp and only quieted when he set her on her feet. He kept a firm hold on her arm, though, holding her close to him when she would have bolted for the wall of fire.

The cold in Alison's body suddenly turned to heat, as if her blood were now molten, thick and boiling, churning in her veins. She wrapped one arm around her stomach and groaned.

Alison?

I'll be all right. She whispered reassurances into his mind and prayed she was telling the truth. But right now, all she felt was a terrible dread building within her. Encompassing all she was, all she'd ever been.

Forcing herself to move, Alison went to her sister, caught her face in her hands and said, "It's time to take me to your boss, Casey. You ready to do that?"

"Balam..." The crooning was back, and that sighing singsong voice rose in the room like a dark prayer.

Aly lifted her gaze to Rogan and didn't want to

think about the fact that his face wasn't clear to her anymore, that all she saw was a blurred image in the shadowy light. "Then let's go."

"You'll stay near me," he warned. "It's too easy by far to be confused in a demon dimension."

"Right with you, I swear." She took a fierce grip on her own dagger, and with Casey between them Aly and Rogan entered the wall of flame.

She couldn't breathe.

The heat was blistering, the brightness blinding. All around her, flames licked at her face, hair and skin, and yet she didn't burn. The heat felt as though it was melting the flesh off her bones. The pain was incredible, and yet her body remained intact—and she wondered then if this was where the legendary descriptions of hell had originated.

Eternal fire. Eternal damnation.

Eternal pain.

You must keep moving, Rogan urged. *If you remain still in the wall of fire, you will die.*

I understand.

And who would have stood still under such blistering, scorching torture? Moving one foot after the other, she went on and on. She felt more than saw Rogan close by. His mind reached for hers, soothing even as they walked deeper into the torment. The flames seemed to stretch on forever with no end in sight. Aly fought her own fears and the slinking sensation of evil that continued to creep through her system.

The fruit she'd eaten would keep her alive in the dimension. But what was it doing to her mind? Was she becoming like Casey?

Would she turn on Rogan her first chance?

Would she lose herself to the darkness that had already claimed her sister?

Hold on to me. Rogan's voice in her mind steadied her, calmed her. She felt his strength, his will, filling her, drowning out her own doubts and fears. *I am with you. Always.*

Rogan... She clung to him. To his courage, his unwavering valor and his love for her. And Aly knew that with him at her side, she could face anything.

On the other side of the flames, Rogan knew instantly that danger surrounded them. The heat still smoldered in his veins, his heart still crashed in his chest and his raging fury still half blinded him. But as they stepped out of the eternal fire, Rogan felt a calmness settle over him, as well.

He had Alison with him, and she would be protected no matter what else happened. Stepping out before her and her sister, he lifted his sword in both hands and held it, point skyward, in front of his chest. His gaze swept the hideously contorted demon dimension and found the threats closest to him.

Scaled demons skittered back and forth ahead of him like pony-size reptiles. Their heads swiveled from side to side with a slow, sure motion, and their claws scraped at the red earth beneath them. The sky was black with no stars to lighten the darkness. There was a moon, but it was blood-red and gave little light.

Around them tall trees squirmed toward that blackness with twisted, writhing limbs, and the flames that burned at their roots blistered but did not consume. The flashing, flickering light of the fires threw ghostly shadows across everything, and Rogan felt Aly's fear mounting.

Defend yourself, he warned, already turning to face a group of former humans, who approached with a blank expression carved on their features. They'd become no better than the demons who scrabbled about on the ground, hissing and clacking their great teeth in a sort of mindless rhythm.

Rogan, maybe those people can be saved, too.

He didn't think so. There were some humans so drawn to their own darkness that if offered true evil would soak it up like a dry sponge. But for her, he would try.

Stay here. First he had to make sure those creatures didn't come too near to Alison.

Rogan inhaled deeply and let loose with a war cry that had once shattered the fighting spirits of his king's enemies. He ran toward the humans and bowled them over like so many pins at the end of an alley. They rolled away from him, and when he sprang at them, knocking first one, then another, insensible with the heavy hilt of his sword, they backed off farther, more than eager to let the demons finish him off.

And there were dozens of demons. Maybe more. In the midst of the battle, Rogan felt Alison's inner struggle for control. He felt her fighting to remain herself in spite of that damn fruit she'd consumed.

He fed the helpless fury by destroying as many of his enemies as he could reach. His sword sliced through the air, his left hand wielding a wicked dagger with unerring accuracy. Demon after demon fell before his blades, and yet there was always another to take its place.

"Rogan! Over here!"

He whirled around at the sound of Alison's voice with a blinding blur of lethal speed. Her fear had prompted her scream instead of a mental call, and he responded instantly.

Her sister, Casey, had scuttled off, disappearing into the crowd. Alison was surrounded by both demons and turned humans. The dagger she held was dark with blood that dripped off the point in a steady, thickening stream. As she waved and jabbed and stabbed with it, her enemies dodged and swayed, moving around her in an ever-shrinking circle.

They were systematically moving in on her.

Closing the circle until she would find no way out, until she was theirs. The demons prowled on all fours, their teeth dripping saliva. The humans under Balam's compulsion moved stiffly but surely, tracking Alison's every movement.

Rogan slammed into those beings standing between him and the woman he loved. Swiping his blades to either side of him, he created a path where none had been, and he didn't stop until he was directly in front of her. "Back, you bastards. You'll fight me and leave the woman."

"You think to give orders in my domain, Guardian?"

Everything stopped. The screams, the fighting. Injured demons slunk away, whimpering. The hot, putrid air felt thick, and malice hung overhead like a cloud.

Rogan straightened to his full, intimidating height and deliberately pushed Alison behind him. A solitary being walked toward him, as the crowd of demons and humans parted way for him like the tide receding from shore.

The demon was tall. Nearly as tall as Rogan, and its yellow eyes caught the light of the fires and glittered dangerously. Its brick-red skin was smooth without scales or hair. It wore black—shirt and pants—which surprised Rogan, somehow. He hadn't thought a demon would be worried about being clothed.

Balam's face was wide and four curved horns, two on each side, jutted out from the back of its head. When it smiled, its sharp, jagged teeth flashed.

"You'd be Balam, I take it," Rogan said.

"I would." The voice was music to its followers, who turned their faces to it in adoration. But its measuring gaze never left Rogan. "And you would be unwelcome, if not unexpected, Guardian."

The demon waved both arms wide, its clawed hands spearing the air with a dramatic flourish. "You risk much in coming here."

Rogan swung his sword in a wide arc, reminding the little demon who'd slipped up on him that he was alert enough to kill and talk at the same time. When Balam laughed, Rogan spared it a look. "You've been hunting in my world, demon. It will stop."

"No, it will not." Balam leaped onto a rock and looked down at the crowd watching it. "Every day, my army swells. You are but one Guardian and cannot think to stop me."

Rogan moved to one side, mentally ordering Alison to keep pace. When she did, he thought no more about it, focusing solely on the demon.

"I can and I will," Rogan shouted, making sure all gathered there heard him.

"Your strength is no match for my power,"

There were scuttling sounds in the fire-bright

darkness. Weeping from a human fighting the turn. The snap and clatter of demon claws. Rogan narrowed his gaze on the demon while constantly aware of what was happening around him.

The others had fallen back, trusting their master to end this. And Rogan was pleased. The creatures under Balam's dominion would scatter like cockroaches once their leader was dead. Rogan had only to kill the one to defeat them all.

"Why take the humans?" Rogan asked, not really caring, wanting only to keep the demon talking, off its guard.

"They can go where my demons cannot. They infiltrate your world and bring me more like them." Sighing with pleasure, the demon looked at those it had created with the pride of a father for his children. "And just see how they thrive here, Guardian. They're more like me than you think."

Rogan... Alison's voice whispered into his mind, shaken, fear-filled. *Something's happening to me.*

He reached for her, wanting to soothe her, but the demon caught his worried frown. "See," Balam continued, "even your woman turns to me. As is right."

In a blink Alison slipped past him, darting beneath the arm Rogan reached out to stop her. Her gaze locked on the demon, she walked toward it with slow, steady steps.

"Alison, stop!" Rogan's shout roared into the air

and brought several of the demons to their knees, cringing at the strength of it. But Alison didn't falter. As if she hadn't heard him at all, she walked on. *Go no farther.* The words were snapped into her mind, but they made no impression on her at all.

The bloody damn fruit had kicked in. It was turning her as it had turned her sister and all the miserable mortals around them. Rogan reached out his senses and knew, as a wave of black thoughts rolled toward him, that he was truly alone now. None of the captured would help. Even those who still fought the turn, like Alison, were too tangled in the demon's web.

As it had been through the centuries, he would face yet another solo battle. Guardian to demon. But the stakes had never been higher for him. Should he lose, not only was he lost but Alison as well. And *that* he would never allow to happen.

Heart frozen in his chest, Rogan bounded after her. And as Balam reached down to snag her arm, Rogan made the leap that landed him on the boulder beside the demon. He swung his sword down in a blindingly fast arc and severed the demon's hand before it could touch Alison.

Balam's howl of pain-laced fury split the night, tearing at the mind, shredding the soul. Rogan brought his sword around again, intending to stab the demon through, but the demon was too fast, leaping down from its perch to stand behind Alison, with one long arm snaked around her throat.

Rogan stilled in the middle of the chaos bursting around him. Demons cheered and shrieked in pleasure. A few of the human captives wailed as if unbelieving of the nightmare they'd found themselves in. But all Rogan could see was Alison.

Her eyes were blank, as if she was no longer in control of her mind, her soul. Her body was stiff and didn't fight back as Balam craned its neck around to scrape its long teeth across her neck in a parody of a caress.

"Take your hand from her or you'll not have any left."

Balam's golden eyes went to slits of pure malice. "You'll pay for taking my hand, Guardian." Slowly, it lifted its injured arm and let black blood pour across Alison's shoulder. "You shouldn't have come here, shouldn't have tried to stop me."

Rogan tried to search Alison's mind, hoping to find a spark where she remained. But her thoughts were closed to him. As though the demon fruit had shut her down completely, making her answerable only to Balam.

"She is mine, Guardian. Like all the others." When the demon lifted its head to stare at Rogan, it smiled, then grabbed Alison's chin with its long fingers. "Join us," it crooned, that too beautiful voice enticing, beguiling. "A Guardian serving me would make me invincible."

"I destroy your kind," Rogan said affably, belying

the terror nestled in a corner of his heart. Alison was gone from him. Her thoughts were shuttered and her eyes were vacant. He must kill the demon no matter what happened to him. She *must* live.

"This one means something to you, does it not?" Balam asked, leaning in and out from behind Alison's head, yellow eyes fixed on Rogan.

"Leave her be, demon."

"Or you will do what?" Balam chuckled and dropped its hand to the base of Alison's throat. Waving the stump of its arm, the demon chided, "This hand will grow back. You think to wound me? Impossible. You think to defeat me? You and your kind are no more than annoyances. I am legion. I am forever."

Rogan inched closer. Keeping his movements so slight they were barely detectable, he strived to get into striking distance.

"I could snap her neck in a blink," the demon sneered, long, clawed fingers tightening on Alison's chin. "One twist and it's done. One snap and she's ended."

Rogan's heart felt as a stone. His lungs couldn't draw air. Fear crawled through him and blended with his rage into a dangerous mix. In centuries of battle he'd done his duty, destroying demons because it was the job he'd been charged with. He'd never hated the demons. They were what they were.

But now a vicious loathing swelled inside him.

This demon's death would be a personal victory. Because the demon would kill Alison. It only toyed with her now to enjoy itself. Rogan would have but one chance to save her—and if he missed, then it wouldn't matter what happened in this miserable place.

Because without her nothing would ever matter again.

"Let us end this," Balam said, enfolding Alison's chin in the palm of its big hand.

"Good idea," Alison said as she went deliberately limp in the demon's grip. When her body dropped, she swung around and slammed the dagger she still held into its chest.

Balam screamed as black blood poured down its body. Eyes wide, the demon looked at Alison in stunned disbelief. It shrieked again, but the sound was cut off as one of Rogan's throwing stars lodged in the demon's throat. Gagging, choking, Balam fell to the dirt, its heels drumming on the earth, its arms flailing as if seeking relief that couldn't be found.

Breathing again, heart beating again, Rogan raced to Alison, plucked her up and held her tight.

I'm all right, she told him mentally. *I had to let him think he had me completely.*

You took such a risk, Alison.

It was the only way.

God, I thought I'd lost you. His mouth found

hers, uncaring that they still stood in the demon dimension, surrounded by enemies on every side.

One brief, bright moment passed when they shared a celebratory kiss; then Rogan pulled his head back and looked at her. Her eyes were focused and clear. And he thanked every God he'd ever worshipped.

I'm really okay, Rogan. That sick feeling inside is gone.

Thank the heavens, he said, over and over again. Then, holding her tightly to one side, Rogan looked down at his fallen enemy and watched as life fled those evil yellow eyes.

And lifting his sword in challenge, Rogan next stared down the remaining few demons. In a moment they ran off, destroyed without their leader.

"Casey!" With the immediate threat gone, Aly shouted her sister's name and pushed out of Rogan's grasp. "Where is she? Casey!"

"Here!" Casey called back, then ran toward her, eyes wide and clear—and terrified. "Aly?" She looked around her at the weird landscape, at the scaled beings still scuttling for cover. "Where the hell are we? What's happening?"

"You're okay!" Aly hugged her sister so tightly she was half-afraid she'd crack Casey's ribs. But the relief was overwhelming. Her sister was back. Her eyes were the blue they should be, and the fear on her features told Aly all was going to be normal again.

Assuming they could get out of the dimension. "Rogan, how do we get out?"

"Rogan?" Casey blurted, her gaze shooting to the big man. "The Guardian? What the hell is he doing here? What is going on?"

"Later," Aly snapped, never taking her gaze from Rogan's. "What do we do?"

"You go home," he said. "Take your sister and those others." Rogan jerked his head at the small knot of humans huddling together. "And go."

"What about you?"

He grabbed her and kissed her, then pushed her at Casey. "The only way out for a human is sacrifice, Alison. And that's up to me."

"No." Panic flared as she saw the resignation in his eyes. He'd already distanced himself from her. "No, you can't stay here. You'll be trapped for eternity."

"And you'll be safe—a good trade." He looked around, making sure they were still alone, then shifted his gaze back to Alison. "The other demons won't stay gone long. Balam is dead, but another leader will rise. They'll be back soon. You must be gone."

"I won't leave you." She grabbed at the front of his shirt and fisted her hands in the material. "I won't leave you *again*."

Grinning down at her despite the situation, Rogan took her face in his hands and kissed her hard and long and deep. "You're not leaving me, Alison. I'm letting you go." In the distance a howling cry went up and quavered. "And you must go now."

He grabbed her arm and dragged her to the wall of flame they'd come through when first they'd arrived. "Take them home, Alison. All of them. I'll hold this gate open for you and when you reach the other side, the portal will open to our world."

As he spoke, a small group of mortals came closer, confused, frightened, whispering together. But there were others, Alison noted. Other humans who had so accepted the turn, they'd become more demon than mortal. They slipped away, disappearing into the blackened, charred forest, making the choice to stay rather than return to the human world.

But they didn't concern her. All that mattered now was Rogan and what he was planning to do.

"I knew coming here that this would be the end," he said softly. "Michael and I spoke of it—on the chance that the demon's hold on the mortals would be broken. To release these humans, I must hold the gate of fire open."

Everything in her wept. He had to stand still. Allow the flames to engulf him. He wouldn't survive. Oh, he might live, but in the end he would be wounded so grievously that the demons would claim him, drag him into this dimension and hold him eternally. Torturing him throughout time.

"I don't want to lose you," she said, even while the others came close, more than ready to leave this place.

"You cannot. I'll always love you," he said, and without another word, he stepped into the living flame. Spreading his arms and legs wide, he held the demon gate open with his body and the trapped mortals scurried through.

Aly only stared at him. Read the suffering in his eyes and the cool resolve that held him in place despite the agonies he suffered. How could she leave him to such a fate?

Casey pulled at her, turned her around and finally said, "Don't let this be for nothing, Aly. Do what he wants. Do what he needs."

"God." She swayed, completely broken. "Rogan."

"Now, Aly!" Casey grabbed her hand and pulled her past the Guardian buying their freedom with his life. They ran through the flames and just before they stepped through to freedom, Aly turned back for one more look.

But Rogan was gone.

Consumed.

Chapter 14

The cool, clear night in Ireland was more welcoming than a kiss.

Aly stumbled through the portal on the heels of her sister, and when Casey's arms came around her, she held on tightly for a moment or two. She couldn't believe this was happening. That she'd lost Rogan. That she'd come back from the demon world without him. Heart breaking, soul shattered, Aly finally stepped free of her sister's embrace, took a deep breath and faced the freed captives.

"You're safe now," she said, fighting the tears choking her. Casey grabbed her hand and squeezed, hard. Grateful for the support, Aly kept talking. "You can all go home now. It's over."

"What happened to us?" one of the women asked, rubbing her hands up and down her arms as if trying to reassure herself that she was alive and safe.

"Doesn't matter anymore," Aly told them and heard her voice break. "The important thing is you're back."

"Where is that guy?" Another woman spoke up. "The one who got us out. Where is he?"

"He…died," Aly made herself say. The words didn't feel real, though. How could an Immortal die? Maybe he was still alive over there. Maybe there was still a chance he could get out, come back to her. Or—her heart gave a leap—she could go back for him. On that thought, she spun around to look at the now-closed portal and realized that there was no way for her to reopen it. Without a Guardian or a demon, that gateway was closed to her.

Rogan was lost.

And she was empty.

"Look," one of the men said as he stepped forward out of the cluster of people. He glanced back at the others, then turned his gaze to Aly. "Uh, we're grateful. And, we won't say anything about this. About any of it."

"Good," Aly said, lifting her chin, standing proud of the man she loved. The man she'd lost.

"Nobody'd believe us anyway, right?" he said on a broken laugh.

The wind whistled through the ruined keep, and it seemed as if the ghosts of the past were rising up in the moonstruck dark. A shiver danced down Aly's spine, and she hunched into herself, tightening her hold on Casey's hand as if that grip were the only thing holding her together.

Slowly, as if they weren't sure where to go or what to do next, the small group of freed captives wandered down the hill to the road. Aly couldn't even care where they went, what they did. How could she care about anything?

"I can't believe he's gone," she whispered.

"Maybe he's not," Casey said, going down on one knee as Aly dropped to the damp ground. "Maybe he can still get out…"

White light exploded all around them, the intensity so brilliant, so clear that Aly and Casey both had to shield their eyes.

When they opened their eyes again, a lone man stood in the clearing, watching them.

"No. Freaking. Way." Casey scrambled to her feet, shaking her head. "No more demons."

"Stop," Aly said, standing up and holding one hand out to her sister. "He's not a demon. He's Michael."

"Michael?"

"Are you well?" Michael asked, sparing a quick look at Casey but concentrating fully on Alison.

"No," Aly snapped, her fear and desperation coloring her voice, "of course I'm not. Rogan's still in there. In the demon world."

Around them, the wind picked up, its icy fingers plucking at her sweater, tossing her hair into a wild tangle at her shoulders. The clarity of the light surrounding Michael nearly blinded her, but she couldn't look away.

"He saved us," Casey said, taking a stand beside her sister. "And all of the others. He showed me something else, too. I'm done being on the sidelines. I want to help end those demons. When we get home, I'm joining the Society. I'll do whatever I can to help. Because of him."

"That's very good," Michael said, though he kept his gaze locked on Aly.

Ignoring the conversation, Aly said the only thing that was important to her.

"Rogan's gone. You have to go in and get him. Save him."

"Definitely," Casey added. "We owe him."

Michael looked down at Aly, and the grief in his eyes froze her to the bone. "The Rogan you knew is no more."

She staggered. "He…he…"

"You must leave this place," he added softly.

"Go home, Alison. Put this behind you. It's what Rogan wanted for you."

Aly rocked in place, feeling the punch of speaking about Rogan in the past tense as if it were a physical blow. Home? How could she go home to Chicago with her heart still rooted firmly here, in Ireland?

As if he knew exactly what she was thinking, Michael gave her a sad smile. "It's all you can do, now. This is done."

"No…" One word, carrying the pain, the misery that would be with her the rest of her life.

"Take the life he gave you," Michael said, the light surrounding him growing more brilliant, more radiant. "And know that I will keep my promise to Rogan and watch over you always."

Then he was gone, and in the darkness Aly clung to her sister and surrendered to desolation.

Aly was a walking dead woman.

She moved and talked and did everything she was supposed to do, but inside she felt as though her heart had been torn from her chest.

The cab ride from O'Hare Airport seemed to last forever. Traffic stalled, the taxi's radio blared rap music and all around her the city bustled with life. It was almost surreal. Only the day before, she'd been in a quiet village on the shores of a lough. She'd survived a demon dimension, lost the only man she'd ever loved and come home to a world that had gone about its business as if nothing had changed.

But that wasn't entirely true. Casey had changed dramatically. Her experience in the demon world was still with her, and she was far different now than she'd been on their trip to Ireland. Quieter, more reflective, she'd consoled Aly and had nearly refused to go to her own home, wanting instead to be with Aly.

But Alison wanted only to be alone. After dropping Casey off at her apartment, the cab driver continued on and finally drove down Aly's long, wide street in Oak Park. The trees reached for each other from both sides of the street, forming a deep green arch that reminded her too much of Ireland. The familiar neighborhood felt strange to her, as if she didn't belong there anymore.

But without Rogan she didn't really belong *anywhere*.

When the taxi stopped, Aly paid him, then got out and waited for her luggage to be set on the curb. She watched the cab drive off and only then turned to look at her house.

The world stopped.

Rogan Butler sat on the front steps of her narrow brick house.

"Rogan?" Hallucinations, she told herself. Her mind refused to accept reality, and now she was going to be seeing him everywhere. Which was, she admitted silently, better than never seeing him again at all.

I'm here.

His voice sang into her mind, and Aly's heart jolted into life again. She took one step. Two. And stopped. Shaking her head, she finally managed to ask, "How?"

He smiled and held up his right hand, palm out. A thin trickle of blood snaked along his skin. "I cut myself on your porch railing." He looked at the blood, then shifted his gaze to hers again and shrugged massive shoulders. "It hasn't stopped bleeding yet, which can only mean I'm human."

Aly laughed shortly, slapped one hand to her mouth to stop what she was afraid would turn into escalating hysteria and stared at him through tear-blurred eyes. "Human? Alive?"

He stood up and she took in all of him, the black leather pants, the long-sleeved black shirt hugging his broad chest and the way his long hair lay loose on his shoulders. His green eyes were filled with love as he watched her.

The tears spilling from her rained unchecked down her cheeks. She couldn't bear to wipe them away, scared that if she rubbed her eyes, he'd some- how disappear.

"But I looked back. Just as we got through the flames, I looked back. You were gone." She forced that last word out on the memory of the pain lancing through her.

He took a single step toward her and stopped. "I was. I woke up in Ireland, with Michael bending over me." He scraped one hand across his jaw. "Surprised the hell out of me. I'd thought to wake up to the demons. Instead…"

"Yes…"

"Michael told me that my 'sacrifice' had worked—you were all safe. But there was more. As it turns out, I wasn't sacrificing my life but my immortality."

More tears, and Aly half wondered if they would ever stop. Hope rose up inside her like a blossoming rose, petals unfurling, spilling light into darkness, happiness into misery. But she was so very afraid to believe.

In a few long strides, Rogan was beside her, touching her, running his big hands up and down her arms and, finally, lifting them to cup her face in his palms. "No more tears, love. We're here. Together."

She lifted both hands and held on to his, frantically blinking to clear her vision, to see his face more clearly.

"I'm as human as you are, Alison." His eyes glowed with light and promise and love. "I want you to marry me. Marry me and return home with me. To Ireland."

"Rogan…"

"I'm no longer a Guardian, Alison. There'll be no more demon fights for me." He gave her a quick smile and another eloquent shrug of his wide shoulders. "I'm to take over the Society Library in Dublin, of all things. All those years of complaining about the bloody Society, and now I'm to be one of you."

She laughed and it felt strange. Wonderful. It was a miracle. All of this was a miracle. And she was terrified that it was a dream from which she'd wake up.

"Come with me," he said, leaning down to her, planting one, then two brief kisses on her upturned mouth. "Love me. Give us the chance we lost so long ago."

"I do love you," she said on a choked sob.

"For centuries," Rogan told her, his voice a hushed groan of need and want, "I was empty. Alone. I filled my days and my nights with the battles that had become neverending. I was a warrior without a soul. All I had was my honor and the duty of fulfilling a vow I made so long ago." He bent, kissed her forehead reverently and whispered, "That vow has been satisfied. Now I'm free to love you. To make a home. A family with you. To show you always how much I love you."

She turned her face into his palm and kissed it.

"We're meant to be together, Alison. And my

love for you, *is* immortal. There is no end to it. Ever."

"Rogan, I love you so much. I was so empty without you, so terrified of living in a world that you'd left." She looked up at him and lost herself in his eyes as she accepted the enormous gift the Fates had granted them. A second chance. A lifetime together. Their promise of eternal love finally fulfilled. "And I will go with you, anywhere."

"That's my love," he said and swept her into his arms. His mouth came down on hers, ravishing, claiming, demanding. And she gave him all she was and more. She gave him her past, her present, her future.

And knew that in him she had found the only home she would ever want.

* * * * *

Don't miss Maureen Child's next release,
SEDUCED INTO A PAPER MARRIAGE,
available in June 2009 from Silhouette Desire.

Harlequin is 60 years old,
and Harlequin Blaze is celebrating!
After all, a lot can happen in 60 years,
or 60 minutes...or 60 seconds!
Find out what's going down in Blaze's
heart-stopping new miniseries,
FROM 0 TO 60!
Getting from "Hello" to "How was it?"
can happen fast....

Here's a sneak peek of the first book,
A LONG, HARD RIDE
by Alison Kent.
Available March 2009.

"IS THAT FOR ME?" Trey asked.

Cardin Worth cocked her head to the side and considered how much better the day already seemed. "Good morning to you, too."

When she didn't hold out the second cup of coffee for him to take, he came closer. She sipped from her heavy white mug, hiding her grin and her giddy rush of nerves behind it.

But when he stopped in front of her, she made the mistake of lowering her gaze from his face to the exposed strip of his chest. It was either give him his cup of coffee or bury her nose against him and breathe in. She remembered so clearly how he smelled. How he tasted.

She gave him his coffee.

After taking a quick gulp, he smiled and said, "Good morning, Cardin. I hope the floor wasn't too hard for you."

The hardness of the floor hadn't been the problem. She shook her head. "Are you kidding? I slept like a baby, swaddled in my sleeping bag."

"In my sleeping bag, you mean."

If he wanted to get technical, yeah. "Thanks for the loaner. It made sleeping on the floor almost bearable." As had the warmth of his spooned body, she thought, then quickly changed the subject. "I saw you have a loaf of bread and some eggs. Would you like me to cook breakfast?"

He lowered his coffee mug slowly, his gaze as warm as the sun on her shoulders, as the ceramic heating her hands. "I didn't bring you out here to wait on me."

"You didn't bring me out here at all. I volunteered to come."

"To help me get ready for the race. Not to serve me."

"It's just breakfast, Trey. And coffee." Even if last night it had been more. Even if the way he was looking at her made her want to climb back into that sleeping bag. "I work much better when my stomach's not growling. I thought it might be the same for you."

"It is, but I'll cook. You made the coffee."

"That's because I can't work at all without caffeine."

"If I'd known that, I would've put on a pot as soon I got up."

"What time *did* you get up?" Judging by the

sun's position, she swore it couldn't be any later than seven now. And, yeah, they'd agreed to start working at six.

"Maybe four?" he guessed, giving her a lazy smile.

"But it was almost two…" She let the sentence dangle, finishing the thought privately. She was quite sure he knew exactly what time they'd finally fallen asleep after he'd made love to her.

The question facing her now was where did this relationship—if you could even call it *that*—go from here?

* * * * *

*Cardin and Trey are about to find out that
great sex is only the beginning….
Don't miss the fireworks!
Get ready for
A LONG, HARD RIDE
by Alison Kent.
Available March 2009,
wherever Blaze books are sold.*

CELEBRATE
60 YEARS
OF PURE READING PLEASURE
WITH HARLEQUIN®!

**We'll be spotlighting a different series
every month throughout 2009
to celebrate our 60th anniversary.**

Look for Harlequin® Blaze™ in March!

0-60

*After all, a lot can happen in 60 years,
or 60 minutes...or 60 seconds!*

Find out what's going down in Blaze's
heart-stopping new miniseries *0-60!*
Getting from "Hello" to "How was it?"
can happen fast....

Look for the brand-new 0-60 miniseries in March 2009!

www.eHarlequin.com   HBRIDE09

You're invited to join our Tell Harlequin Reader Panel!

By joining our new reader panel you will:

- Receive Harlequin® books—they are FREE and yours to keep with no obligation to purchase anything!
- Participate in fun online surveys
- Exchange opinions and ideas with women just like you
- Have a say in our new book ideas and help us publish the best in women's fiction

In addition, you will have a chance to win great prizes and receive special gifts!
See Web site for details. Some conditions apply.
Space is limited.

To join, visit us at
www.TellHarlequin.com.

REQUEST YOUR FREE BOOKS!

2 FREE NOVELS PLUS 2 FREE GIFTS!

Silhouette®

nocturne™

Dramatic and Sensual Tales of Paranormal Romance.

YES! Please send me 2 FREE Silhouette® Nocturne™ novels and my 2 FREE gifts (gifts are worth about $10). After receiving them, if I don't wish to receive any more books, I can return the shipping statement marked "cancel." If I don't cancel, I will receive 4 brand-new novels every other month and be billed just $4.47 per book in the U.S. or $4.99 per book in Canada, plus 25¢ shipping and handling per book plus applicable taxes, if any*. That's a savings of about 15% off the cover price! I understand that accepting the 2 free books and gifts places me under no obligation to buy anything. I can always return a shipment and cancel at any time. Even if I never buy another book from Silhouette, the two free books and gifts are mine to keep forever.

238 SDN ELS4 338 SDN ELXG

Name _____ (PLEASE PRINT)

Address _____ Apt. #

City _____ State/Prov. _____ Zip/Postal Code

Signature (if under 18, a parent or guardian must sign)

Mail to the Silhouette Reader Service:
IN U.S.A.: P.O. Box 1867, Buffalo, NY 14240-1867
IN CANADA: P.O. Box 609, Fort Erie, Ontario L2A 5X3

Not valid to current subscribers of Silhouette Nocturne books.

Want to try two free books from another line?
Call 1-800-873-8635 or visit www.morefreebooks.com.

* Terms and prices subject to change without notice. N.Y. residents add applicable sales tax. Canadian residents will be charged applicable provincial taxes and GST. Offer not valid in Quebec. This offer is limited to one order per household. All orders subject to approval. Credit or debit balances in a customer's account(s) may be offset by any other outstanding balance owed by or to the customer. Please allow 4 to 6 weeks for delivery. Offer available while quantities last.

Your Privacy: Silhouette is committed to protecting your privacy. Our Privacy Policy is available online at www.eHarlequin.com or upon request from the Reader Service. From time to time we make our lists of customers available to reputable third parties who may have a product or service of interest to you. If you would prefer we not share your name and address, please check here. ☐

SN08R

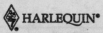

nocturne™

COMING NEXT MONTH

#59 IMMORTAL BRIDE • Lisa Childs

Guilt-stricken Damien Gray believes he is losing his mind—everywhere he turns he sees the spirit of his beautiful bride, Olivia, whose disappearance is a mystery. Not willing to lose her again, he seeks to find a way to connect the divide between the living and the dead. But first he must battle an evil presence in the ghost realm, who is determined to ensure Damien never finds true happiness....

#60 FURY CALLS • Caridad Piñeiro

The Calling

When Blake Richards made the choice to turn Meghan Thomas into one of the undead, he hadn't realized just how angry she would be—even after four years! To win back her love, Blake must show her he's no longer the rogue she knew. But when a deadly feeding frenzy overcomes their vampire clientele, can he convince her that he isn't somehow involved?